THE UNKNOWN COLLABORATOR
AND OTHER LEGENDARY TALES

VINCENT-VICTOR JOLY (1807-1870), was born in Brussels where, in the 1830s, he built his reputation as a journalist and playwright, cultivating a strong interest in Belgian history and legendary episodes, which he dramatized in several plays and a number of short novels. He also published tourist guides to his homeland. The last of his works of fiction was *Histoires ténébreueses* [Dark Stories], here translated as *The Unknown Collaborator and Other Legendary Tales*. The title story is a fine Faustian fantasy, and "The End of a Story of which the Beginning is Familiar" is a highly original fantasy featuring the seven-league boots of legend.

BRIAN STABLEFORD has been publishing fiction and non-fiction for fifty years. His fiction includes a series of "tales of the biotech revolution" and a series of metaphysical fantasies featuring Edgar Poe's Auguste Dupin. He is presently researching a history of French *roman scientifique* from 1700-1939 for Black Coat Press, translating much of the relevant material into English for the first time, and also translates material from the Decadent and Symbolist Movements.

VICTOR JOLY

THE UNKNOWN COLLABORATOR
AND OTHER LEGENDARY TALES

Translated and with an Introduction by

BRIAN STABLEFORD

CONTENTS

Introduction *vii*

The Unknown Collaborator *3*
The End of a Story of which the Beginning is Familiar *69*
A Nocturnal Visit *119*
The Death of Guillaume d'Aremberg de la Marck, known as the Wild Boar of the Ardennes *133*

INTRODUCTION

HISTOIRES TÉNÉBREUSES by Victor Joly, here translated as *The Unknown Collaborator and Other Legendary Tales*, was first published in Brussels by Auguste Schnee & Co. in 1857. It collects three novellas and a short story, all affiliated, albeit a trifle belatedly and more than a little ironically, to the Romantic Movements of France and Germany, fusing the two influences in a fashion that only a Belgian writer was likely to attempt, and thus producing a hybrid whose distinctiveness is particularly obvious in the first two stories in the collection, each of which makes a significant contribution to the rich tradition of Romantic satanic fantasies.

Vincent-Victor Joly (1807-1870) began his literary career as a journalist and playwright. The record of his journalistic work is presently rather scanty, few Belgian periodicals of the period having yet been scanned for on-line access, but court records indicate that in 1833 he was the editor of a periodical entitled *Le Sancho*, in which capacity he incurred a punitive fine as a result of a complaint of defamation made by one Henri Cabry, presumably having tilted at the wrong windmill. As a playwright he launched his endeavors with *Le Juif errant: mystification fantastique en trois tableaux* [The Wandering Jew: A Fantastic Mystification in Three Scenes], performed at the Théâtre des Folies Dramatiques in 1834, and published the same year under the pseudonym "M. Jacob." He followed it up with *Jacques Artevelde, drame en trois actes et en sept tableaux* [Jacques Artevelde; A Drama a Three Acts and Seven Scenes], published under his own name a year later.

The latter work was preceded in its published version by a long prose section of "Chroniques Flamandes" [Flemish Chronicles] filling in the fourteenth-century background to the historical drama, and that endeavor indicated the principal direction his subsequent work was to take. He became a passionate researcher and dramatizer of the history of his native Belgium, with which almost all of his later work deals. That focus narrowed the potential scope of his celebrity considerably, being problematic even within his homeland, where only half the population shared his predilection for the French language.

One copy of the play *Le Bourgeois de Gand, ou Le Secrétaire du duc d'Albe* [The Burger of Ghent; or, The Duke of Alba's Secretary] (1838), which was produced at the Odéon in Paris, although published in Brussels, where it is set, is attributed to Joly by Google Books, although its signature, Hippolyte Romand, is recorded by the Bibliothèque Nationale as that of a real individual and the false attribution is presumably an error. A biographical note written by Felix Delhasse in 1839, however, credits Joly with contributions to the *Chronique de Paris* and *Le Siècle*, so he might well have been in France for some time in the late 1830s, and his unpublished play *Gonsalve, ou Les proscrits* [Gonsalves; or, The Exiles] (1837) is said by Delhasse to have been produced in Lyon and Marseilles before being staged in his naïve Brussels. Joly seems, however, to have concentrated almost entirely on prose works thereafter, including the historical novellas *Siège de Maestricht, sous Alexandre Farnèse, duc de Parma en 1579* [The Siege of Maastricht by Alexander Farnese, Duke of Parma, in 1579] (1840), *Une tuerie au XVIe siècle* [A Sixteenth-Century Massacre] (1841) and *Jean de Weert: Une nuit de Noël sous Philippe II* [Jean de Weert: A Christmas Eve during the Reign of Philippe II] (1842).

Joly also produced tourist guide-books to Belgium and the Ardennes, and his journalistic work also included art criticism, which led to his publication of a study of *Les Beaux-arts en Belgique de 1848-1857* [The Fine Arts in Belgium from 1848-1857] (1857). The latter was published in the same year as *Histoires ténébreuses*, and the two books appear to have been the last ones he published, although he was only fifty at the time and lived for another thirteen years.

The original version of *Histoires ténébreuses* begins with "La Mort de Guillaume d'Aremberg de la Marck, dit le *Sanglier des Ardennes*," the translation of which I have relocated as the fourth item in the present volume. It was presumably placed first in the original because it is in much the same vein as his earlier historical novellas, albeit somewhat darker in tone and more straightforward in its admission that it is dealing with legend rather than established fact. It is also fringed with quasi-supernatural references, which link it more closely with the other stories in the volume. In that respect, the shortest story in the volume, "Une Visite nocturne," only flatters in order to deceive, but the two novellas that I have placed first and second are full-blown stories of the supernatural that might well indicate a new direction that the author had begun to take in his work—or to which he had reverted, although *Le Juif errant* is only obliquely based on the legend of that individual's alleged sighting in Brussels in 1774—before fading from the view of history himself.

If the implications of "Une Visite nocturne" can be trusted—and the evidence of the other stories certainly supports the supposition—Joly had once been a very enthusiastic reader of Romantic and Gothic fiction, with a particular fondness for Faustian fantasies, including Lord Byron's *Manfred* as well as Goethe's *Faust*, and although he seems to have looked back subsequently on that fascination with a certain wry shame, it is not really surprising that he should have made ventures of his own in that direction. Evidently able to read English, Dutch and German as well as French, he probably had a syncretic view of the produce of Romanticism that was unusually coherent as well as unusually broad, and was certainly aware of a degree of tension between the typical French Romantic attitude to supernatural materials and the typical German attitude: a tension of which he makes considerable use in his two supernatural novellas.

"Un Collaborateur inconnu" belongs to a rich tradition of French Romantic fantasies, in many of which the image of Satan is drastically and ironically reconfigured, to the extent that the most ideologically extreme contributions to the subgenre, including Alfred de Vigny's "Eloa" (1824) and Alphonse de Lamartine's "La Chute d'un ange" [An Angel's Fall] (1832-33) can be given credit for launching the tradition of literary Satanism that was eventually to produce such masterpieces as Gustave Flaubert's *La Tentation de Saint Antoine* (1874, although an earlier version, written in 1849, was published subsequently; tr. as *The Temptation of Saint Anthony*) and Anatole France's "L'Humaine tragédie" (1895; tr. as "The Human Tragedy"). Joly's Germany-set story certainly does not go to the extent of cultivating sympathy for Satan, but it does present an unusual and original image of the tactics of temptation, and suggests a role for the demon in human affairs and human history that concedes him a far more Romantic role than traditional representations imply.

Amusing as it would have been in 1857, it is arguable that the ironic component of "Un Collaborateur inconnu" has gained an extra twist in the interim by virtue of its notion of what the perfect temptation for an ambitious German Romantic poet might consist, and the author deserves credit for both perception and a measure of ironic anticipation. Joly's story also makes for an interesting comparison with the two Satanic novelettes in Charles Asselineau's near-contemporary collection *Le Double vie* (1858; tr. as *The Double Life*), which similarly deal with the other side of the diabolical coin in reconfiguring torment as well as temptation in the same ironic spirit.

"Fin d'une histoire dont le commencement est bien connu" is a considerably more exotic story than "Un Collaborateur inconnu," imaginatively very ambitious in spite of the appropriation of its central motif from a tradition of mock-folkloristic fantastic fiction that is indeed familiar in both French and German versions. It must have seemed rather *avant garde* in 1857, but, like "Un Collaborateur inconnu," it has gained imaginative ground in the interim; its metaphorical account of the activities of the demonic host and its reconfiguration of their relationship with

Heaven has acquired further relevance and satirical bite in the interim. It qualifies as one of the earliest environmentalist fantasies ever penned, all the more remarkable in its satirical acidity by virtue of its pioneering status. Beneath its comical and frankly absurdist surface, it is a remarkably disenchanted story, which, if it reflects the author's thinking accurately, might offer some hint as to the reason for his disappearance from the literary world after its publication. It is, at any rate, a unique work that warrants recognition as an eccentric classic of fantastic fiction.

Histoires ténébreuses was published in the same year as Charles Baudelaire's *Les Fleurs du mal,* in a period when French literature, particularly in its more adventurous endeavors, was subject to a good deal of external stress. The Second Empire had begun in 1852 with a period of exceedingly strict censorship, and many of the leading figures of the Romantic Movement had been exiled because of their Republican sympathies. By 1857 the censorship was beginning to ease up and the exiles had been offered amnesty, but Baudelaire and Gustave Flaubert were both successfully prosecuted for obscenity in that year, and the limits of toleration remained sensitive. Brussels had long been a favorite place of residence for French literary exiles and a favorite place of publication for works that were deemed unpublishable in Paris; Joly was undoubtedly acquainted with some of the exiles and familiar with the significance of his home town as an important outpost of *avant garde* French literary culture.

Although there is no reason to think that the material in *Histoires ténébreuses* could not have been published in Paris, it was nevertheless produced in an intellectual climate that was somewhat adversarial to the forced diplomacy of many of the Romantic writers who remained active in Paris in the 1850s, and Joly was well aware of his entitlement to give freer rein to a spirit of enterprise that had been temporarily damped down in the French capital. That adds a little extra spice to stories that have not received full historical credit for their achievement in France or in Belgium because of their perceived marginality, although they are works of high quality.

This translation was made from the copy of the Schnee edition reproduced on the Bibliothèque Nationale's *gallica* website.

Brian Stableford

THE UNKNOWN COLLABORATOR
AND OTHER LEGENDARY TALES

THE UNKNOWN COLLABORATOR

THE cause has never been sought of the belief that we accord to events and supernatural traditions dating back a century or two, while, on the other hand, we greet with the most extreme skepticism events that are accomplished before our eyes, whose circumstances escape completely the laws of moral and material order. It seems that the fantastic needs to be enveloped in the shadows of the past in order to reach us, and that the glimmering of our disdainful philosophy has been the dawn at the appearance of which all the unusual, bizarre or mysterious things that are the domain of the fantastic vanished.

The location in which one of those events occur that collide with all our acquired ideas, and escape the explanations of our presumptuous science, is not without influence on the degree of faith that we accord to legends of times that are no more. Under the somber oaks of the forests of Franconia, on the sterile and rocky summits of the Hartz, which seem to bear the imprint of some gigantic orgy, in the half-light of the Scottish valleys, sleeping beneath shadows of birch-trees and holly-bushes, the mind accumulates, with a serious and profound faith, all the marvelous legends that bring a smile of disdainful incredulity to the lips in the noisy surroundings of a big city.

You can, therefore, believe what you like of the adventure that we are about to recount, whose hero we met during a visit we made to a hospice for the insane in Cologne a few years ago.

I

In 1832 there was a young man at the university of Heidelberg, the issue of one of those noble families of Germany who strive in vain to hide their proud poverty under the imperfect veil of a deceptive luxury. Ulric R***'s father was typical of the old Swabian barons raised in a profound respect for the antiquity of their family and a hatred of foreigners. He had taken part in the glorious awakening of Germany of which Theodore Körner was the sublime Tyrtaeus.[1] Then, when peace came, he had returned to his Franconian manor and had quivered with joy at the sight of his son Ulric, the memory of whom had appeared to him so frequently in the midst of Germany's heroic struggles between 1813 and 1815.

---

1 Carl Theodor Körner (1791-1813) was a poet who took up arms to fight for the liberation of Germany following its temporary conquest by Napoléon; he joined a militia organized by Ludwig von Lützow, known as the *Schwarze Jäger* [Black Hunters] and was killed in battle. His fervently patriotic and militaristic *Schwertlied* [Sword Song], composed shortly before his death, was set to music by Carl Maria von Weber and became popular in Germany as the emblem of his martyrdom; he was nicknamed "the German Tyrtaeus" after a militaristic Spartan poet.

Ulric's education had been simple and austere. He had learned to read in a single book, the finest and greatest that has ever been offered to human meditation. That magnificent treasure of wisdom and poetry—the Bible—had given young Ulric's mind a character of grandeur and indescribable reverie, which solitude had only augmented. Later, the study of poets such as Goethe, Byron, Shelley and Jean Paul, came to increase that grim melancholy, and at the age when everything smiles upon those who are commencing life, when the heart is radiant and all gilded hopes are hatching in the soul, Ulric already felt a suspension above his head, as if misfortune had touched him with its iron hand.

It is to the influence of that sad literature, the somber poetry that had for the strings of its lyre doubt, despair and revolt against God, to the cries of thunderstruck Titans that resounded in the works of poets twenty years ago, that it is necessary to attribute those sad maladies of the soul, those moral nostalgias that have claimed so many victims in France and Germany.

Germany especially, that soil where the beautiful flowers of azure and the ideal bloom and where the songs of poets resemble the magnetic and vibrant sounds of Aeolian harps, has seen many of its children fall under that accursed breath, which desiccated all hopes, and withered all beliefs and all amours. The ravages have been more profound there than anywhere else. The inclination and nature of the Germanic mind, the aspect of its terrain, covered with ruins from which the voices of the past seem to emerge, its age-old mysterious forests whose echoes sometimes awaken under the fanfares of Palatine counts and accursed hunters, all the way to the old Rhine, ancient

witness to the great German epics—everything, in sum—
augments that thirst for the unknown, that aspiration toward the infinite, which has claimed so many victims and
has drawn so many young intelligences toward the gulf
in the depths of which the demon of despair and suicide
smiles at his prey.

Ulric was, therefore, attained by that strange malady,
which French mockery has succeeded in curing by ridi-
cule, and which Goethe himself combated, after having
been one of the poisoners of souls at whose sufferings
he later jeered. In Ulric, an enervating and somber reverie
had ended up dominating all the mental faculties, which
languished further every day like a vigorous tree attacked
at the heart by a malevolent insect.

In order fully to appreciate all the ravages made in Ulric's mind, it is necessary to understand the influence of
the nature in whose bosom he was born. The great woods
of Franconia, all populated with traditions, and in which
his dreams wandered, had gradually ended up by extracting him from the realities of his life. His existence had
become a kind of mental somnambulism, the first step
toward the profound fall in which his reason was one day
to break.

Ulric's father, a man of action, of positive life and reality, could not comprehend his son's mental state. It was
not that he was deaf to poetic things, but his own poetry
resided in the events that he had seen accomplished before
his eyes. The gigantic struggles against Napoléon, in which
he had taken part, seemed to him then to be as many epics that cast back into the shadows the great Carlovingian
wars. That man of battles, that intrepid companion of the
poet Körner who, when the charge of the Black Hunters

was sounded by Lützow, demanded his inspirations from his saber, understood nothing of the reveries that were devouring his son. In his eyes, the great poets were men of action such as Tilly, Wallenstein, Cortez, Pizarro, Ziska and other elite natures, writing their immortal names with their swords in the annals of nations.

The only point by which Ulric still held on to reality was a frantic, immense desire to equal one of those princes of intelligence and poetry whose names he could not hear without an admiration mingled with envy. He would have given without difficulty all the flowers of his youth, all the pure emotions of his heart and the limpidity of his forehead, for the glory and the furrowed brow of Schiller, Byron, Goethe or Klopstock. Literary renown dominated all others in his eyes. He shivered with joy at the thought of one day seeing his name surrounded by the aureole of glory whose glare eclipsed, in his eyes, all earthly happiness.

Although he had scarcely arrived at the age when others amass by study the future materials that intelligence will one day organize in monuments of science, art or poetry, Ulric, devoured by the fever of renown, had already exercised himself on several subjects that betrayed his poetic references and sympathies. In reading Byron and Schiller, he seemed to feel in his heart the impatience of Job's horse at the sound of clarions. Like the Biblical charger he said to himself: *Let's go!* and his gaze lit up at the voice of his poets of predilection.

There was in that young intelligence a relentless struggle. He felt, at times, great thoughts rising up within him, but which fell back into the darkness as soon as he tried to realize them and fix them in any kind of frame. Eyes turned toward a poetic ideal, which revealed itself to him like a chink of light through a gap in clouds, he strove to attain those divine regions, but just as he reached the threshold, he fell back, crushed by the sentiment of a cruel impotence. A longer struggle would have sufficed to break the most virile spirit, and Ulric's was to succumb as a consequence of an adventure that happened to him in Heidelberg, which we are about to recount.

Ulric's father's fortune had been cruelly dilapidated during the long wars of Germany against France. Reduced to a meager patrimony and a modest pension, the Baron thought one day that it was time to extract his son from the contemplative life that was undermining all the sinews of his soul. He therefore informed him of the state of his fortune and made him understand that the peace that Europe was enjoying was about to open to the young generation a host of careers worthy of the highest ambitions.

"The reign of the sword is over, my son," said the old Baron, "and the saber of Lützow's Black Hunters will not reflect the lightning of battles for a long time. You are young, Ulric, and handsome, and your forehead is radiant with the future. I have told you what remains of the fortune of your forefathers. A ruined manor over which the crows soar, as if they foresaw that they would soon take possession of it—that is the entire heritage that I have to leave you. We are a proud and devoted race, habituated to sell a domain in every war that has menaced Germany. From the height of the towers of this castle, your gaze can embrace all the possessions over which the banner of our ancestors fluttered, but in each of those national struggles the circle has narrowed. We have given the fatherland our gold and our blood, as loyal and faithful children. Today, nothing remains to us, and I foresee, Ulric, that it will be necessary for you to be the architect of your own fortune and reconquer by intelligence what your forefathers have lost by war. I have therefore thought of sending you to Heidelberg, where you can complete your studies while waiting for your wings to be strong enough to bear you toward the summit you have chosen."

That determination of the old baron smiled too much at the young man for him to have the slightest observation to make. It realized one of his cherished dreams. He was about to find himself in company with the leading lights of art, science and thought; he was about to find new sources for his ardent desire to know, and to live side by side with the sun of poetry that made such a beautiful aureole of glory for Germany. He was finally about to realize the great thoughts that tormented his soul like the lava of a volcano whose crater has been filled in, and cast them in the frame of an immortal work.

Rich with a few hundred florins and all the fresh hopes that cover the mountain of life with flowers, Ulric arrived in Heidelberg equipped with a letter of introduction to the son of one of his father's friends, a young man of his own age who was to be his companion in study.

It was night when Ulric, followed by a domestic who was carrying his meager baggage, stopped outside a house of mediocre appearance whose upper windows were illuminated, and from which noisy rumors were emerging: the songs and the outbursts of voices that only half a dozen students in a good mood can produce.

"That's it, Seigneur Student," said the domestic, pointing with his finger to the flamboyant windows, and then he withdrew.

Ulric slowly went up two floors and knocked at the door of the noisy cenacle, in such a fashion as to dominate the noise of the bacchanal taking place inside.

The door, which suddenly opened, showed the young man a curious spectacle. Seven or eight young people were sitting around a table on which a formidable bowl of punch was ablaze, the bright light of which caused the candlelight to pale. A thick cloud of tobacco smoke surrounded the guests with a semi-transparent veil and gave them I know not what appearance of Scandinavian gods enveloped in their robe of fog. Pipes, swords and pistols garnished walls whitened by chalk, on which a few fine engravings by Albrecht Dürer were nailed. On the mantelpiece, a little Venetian glass supported a palm from Palm Sunday. At the back of the room, one of the drinkers was swinging in a hammock, magisterially smoking a long American pipe whose flexible bowl brushed the floor. All the guests had taken off their coats and cravats, and a few were gravely tearing up their classic books in order to light their pipes.

At the sight of Ulric standing on the threshold of the room, a profound silence fell; all gazes turned toward him with a curiosity mingled with slight suspicion. On all the faces of the young men, stimulated by the spur of the punch, there was a confidence and intelligence that impressed Ulric greatly. Those fine German heads, ordinarily inclined beneath the wing of reverie, were radiant at that moment with an irresistible power.

"Which of you, Messieurs, is named Max?" said Ulric, interrogating all the guests with his gaze, while he took a letter out of his braided frock-coat.

"Me," said the smoker in the hammock, raising himself up on his elbow. "If you've come on the part of my banker, may God protect you! If you're the envoy of some Philistine, may the Devil take you!"

"I've come on the part of a friend and I bring words of peace," said Ulric, smiling, as he handed Max the letter of introduction he had in his hand.

"Messieurs," said Max, after having scanned the letter rapidly, "I introduce to you a brother, the son of Baron von R***, one of the brave centaurs of Lützow, who received Körner's last sigh. Someone refill, in honor of our new comrade, the cup of Hercules."

With a bound, Max launched himself out of his hammock and took an immense Bohemian glass from a table, whose capacity could have made Maréchal de Bassompierre himself recoil, who once drank a colossal toast to thirteen Swiss canons from his riding-boot filled with wine.[1]

"To your star and your future glory!" said Max.

The cup, whose enormous proportions seemed to have been created for some hero of the *Nibelungenlied*, made a circuit of the table and returned to Max, who emptied it in one draught.

"Now, brothers, that our new brother has shared with us the bread and salt, and has smoked the universitarian calumet, he is affiliated to the free and joyous congregation of Renards. The session is open, and Franck has the floor."

"What are you discussing, Messieurs?" said Ulric.

"Almost anything," said Max, holding out his glass to the dispenser of drinks. "The discussion has extended

---

1 The reference is to François de Bassompierre (1579-1646), a favorite of Henri IV, whose memoirs became an important historical resource.

over love, liberty, poetry, the waltz in triple time, Rhenish wine, the Turk, revenants, riding-boots and the part the Devil plays in things of this world. You can see brother, that the conversation has breadth. Today we're holding our drinking congress, from which we normally pass on to the scattershot of a free and picturesque discussion of everything that has been and will be.

"So, Messieurs," said the young man to whom Max had given the name of Franck, "I was saying that it is unnecessary to seek any further than the works attributed to the sons of men to find the traces there of the claw of Old Iniquity, as Goethe calls him. A host of monuments, especially those that travelers admire the most and which strike the mind of peoples by their character of colossal grandeur or sublime boldness, have had the Devil for a collaborator. Look at our cathedral of Cologne, which people are striving in vain to finish.[1] Ten successive generations have attempted to complete and conclude the house of the Lord; quests have been undertaken throughout Germany, even kings have drawn upon their treasuries with full hands; nothing has worked. One part falls into ruins while another is edified. The naves crack when towers are elevated. Then too, the original plan is lost. One goes at hazard, like pedants who would like to replace a lost book by Diodorus or fill in the lacunae in Tacitus. Mortar is mixed, stone

---

1 Construction of Cologne Cathedral had begun in 1248 but abandoned in 1473, with the task incomplete. In 1842 work was resumed, in association with the Romantic enthusiasm for the Medieval and the Gothic, employing what was ostensibly, but somewhat controversially, the original plan, but using modern construction methods. Joly could not know that, in spite of many difficulties, the project would eventually be completed in 1880.

is carved, two are placed to the north and three fall down to the south. Go on! There is more truth and philosophy in popular traditions than one might think, and Germany will be returned to its great national unity while Cologne cathedral still raises its truncated towers toward the heavens like an Occidental Babel."

"Do you know, Franck," said Max, smiling, "that you take the part of old Satan very well in permitting him to oppose his veto to the competition of the most beautiful monument of Christianity, the one that was to be a magnificent symbol of the new law?"

"God has permitted him many other things," said Franck, "and seems always to have retained a residue of affection for the one who was once the foremost of his seraphim. Then too, up there it's a little like here. Thus, are not you, Max, who are certainly the blackest sheep in your family, to whom your mother has sent diamonds in secret to pay your debts, who has had your father kill a herd of fatted calves by promising him every time not to squander his fortune, your health and your future any longer, the favorite of all his sons? The last time the worthy man came to see you, I kept him company awaiting your return. Now, I remember that you came back that day mounted on a magnificent horse, which you had just bought without knowing how you would pay for it. Well, do you know what your father said on seeing you?"

"Doubtless he commenced a sermon, or began with some Ciceronian criticism: *Quousque tandem*,[1] etc."

"You're unjust to your worthy father, my dear Max. On seeing you handle your horse in a fashion to make it execute all the equestrian coquetries that please women so

---

1 "For how much longer . . . ?"

much, your father turned to me and said, with the most charming smile: 'Wouldn't my Franck make a fine captain of hussars?' Well, God has a similar weakness for the escapades of his fallen angel; he has permitted him a host of incongruous capers—for instance, the worthy Job, whom he allowed him to torment in so many ways."

"You're forgetting that the patriarch's wife was party to that," said Max, gravely. "Let's not calumniate old Satan. God knows what happened to Luther for having attempted to ruin the Devil's reputation in Germany."

"But we're getting a long way from Cologne cathedral," said Ulric. "I'd like to hear Franck finish what he was telling us about that subject."

"So, I was saying," Franck resumed, "that the architectonic marvels of the world almost all bear the imprint of a superhuman power. Who built those palaces at Baalbeck, each stone of which is seventy feet long and twenty high? Who placed those ceilings of a single block of more than four hundred square feet on hundred-foot columns? Where are the Titans who kneaded the rocks whose fragments serve us to make obelisks?

"Today, when we dispose of steam and gunpowder, and mechanics has made incontestable progress, where are the architects who would dare to undertake to hollow out temples like those of Ellora and Elephanta, monstrous prodigies for which a mountain of granite was disemboweled and carved, temple, column and gods, in the proportions of the Colossus of Rhodes? Ask the Brahmins who the architect was to whom superhuman temples are owed into which no ray of sunlight will ever penetrate, and they will whisper in your ear a terrible and familiar name.

"Now, to get back to our Cologne cathedral, that other weaving of the Penelope of Christianity, do you know what I was told last week by Fritz the carpenter, who works in the forest of the nave?"

"No," said all the guests with attentive expressions.

"This is it: Fritz was singing while squaring off a beam when, all of a sudden, he perceived that he had forgotten his compasses. He was about to go to the door of the attics to call his apprentice when he saw, to his astonishment, that someone had taken away the ladder that replaced a part of the stairway still under construction. He lay down on his front and called to his companion in a loud voice, but the church was deserted and his voice awoke a host of echoes that sent back his words with strange sounds. He shouted again, but in vain. Not one workman was in the church, and his voice, falling from the height of the nave, which is no less than two hundred feet high, might well not have been heard. He therefore returned to the roof-space and opened a window to call for help, but the wind was blowing with such force that he could hardly hear the sound of his voice himself.

"He could see a few workmen at the foot of the monument, but their words reached him as a slight murmur. He made signs and called out, but nothing worked. His apprentice, thinking that he had left, had doubtless taken away the ladder to the roof-space for some other purpose and had thus left his master imprisoned two hundred feet above the ground. Fritz was in a murderous mood, as you can imagine, all the more so as night was approaching and he saw himself threatened with sleeping in the church without any supper.

"Soon, the shadow overtook the city and the last rays of sunlight were gilding the gigantic edifice. The noises down below gradually ceased, and numerous church bells sent him the hours, which traversed the air like sonorous messengers. The city went to sleep, the flamboyant windows gradually winking out, and soon everything was shadow and silence.

"It was necessary to make a decision, whatever it might be, and the wisest thing was to resign himself. Fritz therefore assembled a bed of woodchips, and then, having said his evening prayer, he threw himself down on his improvised bed, where he didn't take long to fall into a profound sleep, promising himself nevertheless to give his apprentice the mighty scolding that that night in an aerial bivouac warranted.

"He had been asleep for two hours when he was woken up by the sound of the bells that were chiming midnight in all the churches. He was turning over on to his other side in order to go back to sleep when he saw a bright light above the well of the stairs to the attics, which lit up the roof and seemed to be coming from the church. Fritz's first thought was that there was a fire in some part of the monument and that he was about to perish, of a horrible death, with no hope of salvation. He got up from his bed precipitately and ran to the opening of the stairway, from which his sight could plunge into the entire church; and he was then struck by the most profound horror, a more mortal fright than if he had seen a sea of fire surrounding him with its devouring waves."

II

At Franck's last words, all the guests had drawn closer to him. He had just touched the favorite cord of the German mind—the fantastic—and all his wide-mouthed listeners were ready to follow him into the increate and vaporous regions of the land of dreams and the unknown.

Franck continued his story thus:

"Through the opening in the vault over which he was lying, facing the interior of the church, Fritz saw things so unexpected and so strange that, in order to assure himself that he was not under the obsession of a monstrous dream, he bit the palm of his hand so violently that the traces of his teeth were still visible there a week later.

"The cathedral doors were open, as if some royal cortege were expected. Soon, Fritz saw little black men appear, possessed of an agility akin to that of monkeys, who spread out like a torrent into the basilica, with the air of hurrying workmen who had come to resume an interrupted task. Almost all of them were wearing the costume of artisans of the fourteenth century: a leather apron circling their loins; from their belt hung chisels, drills, hammers, files and pincers. Those who appeared to be the masons of the bizarre troop had neither trowels nor levels, but little iron levers; tools serving for construction were entirely lacking, but on the other hand, all the instruments of destruction invented by humans were in the hands of those strange workmen.

"The church was increasingly filled by those singular beings, whose footfalls did not awaken any sound under the sonorous vaults. Through the somber arcade of the portal, a dense black crowd could be seen passing, which rose like a living river along the friezes, and over the windows, the workmen's mullions, the ribs, the vaults and the capitals of columns. Then the black swarming waves reached the upper galleries and covered the rose-windows, the trefoils and the pendants with a dark mobile veil. And the legions of workers were still coming in!

"Soon, the vast flanks of the monument, the shafts of high columns, and the ogives of galleries were covered with that singular population, which seemed to have, like bats, the faculty of attaching themselves to flat vertical surfaces. Finally, when the entire church was covered with that infernal living crepe, which decked it as if for some mysterious funeral, a strident and imperious voice was heard beneath the porch, brothers, crying out: '*The Master!*'

"That name, which fell into the midst of the solemn silence that reigned in the cathedral, made Fritz shiver and covered his whole body with a cold sweat. He made the sign of the cross, and closed his eyes in order to tear himself away from the mysteries that were about to be accomplished—but an inexplicable power forced him to be the witness of the strangest thing that has ever struck a Christian's gaze.

"The voice that had announced *the Master* had found an echo in the thousands of workers who filled the nave and the aisles but who, by a singular circumstance, had not been able to cross the railings of the choir. A noise of shrill voices ran through the edifice like a sonorous wave, rose from the floor along the columns, launched by the mullions of windows, and descended via the drops of arches like an animate current. Fritz perceived then that the strange light that was illuminating the nave, which had made him think that there was a fire, was coming from a little flame that each worker bore on top of the head, which was vacillating like the fire follets of cemeteries. However, singularly enough, although the inside of the church was resplendent with light, the windows did not cast any light outside, and the flanks of the monument were enveloped by thick darkness.

"Suddenly, the porch lit up in a dazzling manner, as if a torrent of molten crystal were passing through it, and the individual whose name had just been pronounced by the crowd, with a mysterious terror, appeared.

"It was a young man of strange beauty, all of whose features bore the imprint of an indomitable pride and an inexpressible suffering. His high and vast forehead, over which fell rich brown curls, seemed to be brooding tumultuous thoughts. His veiled gaze, profound and implacable, illuminated the most profound shadow. The corners of his mouth, turned upwards by irony, betrayed an inescapable despair.

"The mysterious individual was clad in a rich velvet costume of antique form, and held in his hand a whip with several thongs, the extremities of which seemed to be armed with spikes. Having arrived at the entrance to the porch, he stopped momentarily, darted a glance radiant with savage irony over the great nave and the lateral naves, closed at their summit by worm-eaten poorly-jointed planks, and then, turning toward the tower on the right, which, in eight centuries, had not been able to rise more than a hundred feet from the ground, he uttered an explosive burst of laughter that seemed to make the colossal monument quiver on its granite foundations.

"While the aisles of the principal nave were inundated with light, the choir and the lateral chapels remained plunged in thick darkness. A single ray of moonlight, traversing the window of the choir, picked out on the window the figure of Saint Hermann and came to illuminate a tumulary stone on which the most piercing eye would have sought an inscription in vain. In the shadow, the white forms appeared of statues of the Queen of Angels and Saint Peter, guarding the entrance to the choir, while the apostles, in their azure robes constellated with flowers and stars, like electors of the Holy Empire, formed a kind of sacred cohort around the columns of the choir. The cold light of the moon, sliding over the tombs of Archbishops Adolf and Anton von Schauenburg, gave their recumbent statues on their marble beds a mysterious appearance of life.

"The unknown, after a few minutes of meditation, during which his gaze wandered over every part of the vast edifice, suddenly advanced toward the choir, the gates of which rotated on their hinges as he approached. The moonbeam that cast its silvery dust on the parvis was eclipsed, as if the sky had been suddenly veiled. The unknown headed toward the tumulary stone with no inscription; then, striking it with his foot imperiously, he said in a menacing voice whose formidable timbre shook the vault: *'Get up! The time has come!'*

"A profound groan responded to that summons, and the cold stone slab slowly rose up, pushed by a specter whose gaze, imprinted with the most profound despair, seemed to be begging the mysterious unknown for mercy.

"The latter replied to that mute supplication with cruel laughter and marched straight to the tomb of the

Archbishops Adolf and Anton, whose statues he struck with a violent whiplash, repeating once again: *'Get up! The time has come!'*

"And the white marble statues got up slowly from their marble beds and came to stand beside the specter of the nameless tomb.

"Then the unknown headed for the tomb of the Archbishops Philipp von Heinsberg and Konrad von Hochstaden, founders of the marvelous cathedral, and struck them with his whip, repeating: *'Get up! Get up! The time has come!'*

"And the stone image of Philipp and the bronze state of Konrad quit their icy couch and came to stand in line next to their mute companions.

"In the meantime, the church filled up with groans and sighs that seemed to be emerging from tombs, but the unknown still went to fustigate with his magic whip all those poor dead men, who shook off their centuries-long sleep, with difficulty, and slowly opened their sepulchers in order to come and stand with their companions.

"Then he marched straight to the ostentatious mausolea of the Princes of Bavaria, buried in front of the chapel of the three Mage Kings who were the first to salute the advent of Christ. And he struck their splendid charnel-houses with his whip, saying, in a terrible voice: 'Get up, princes of the Earth, now vassals of the sepulcher. *Get up! The time has come!'*

"And all those nameless beings, clad in broken crowns, velvet mantles and gold faded by the darkness of the coffin slowly got up and went to stand alongside their dismal subjects.

"The unknown became increasing grim, his voice more

and more menacing, his gaze devouring. He raised his eyes toward the statues of the apostles placed thirty feet from the parvis; twice he raised his redoubtable whip over those companions of Christ, and twice his arm fell back, as if paralyzed by a superior power. Finally, hatred carried him away; he directed his whip at the statue of Saint Peter, repeating his terrible: 'Get up!' The apostle remained motionless in his azure dalmatic.

"Furious, the unknown was about to redouble his effort when he suddenly went pale, on perceiving before him a golden shield borne by an invisible arm, the glare of which was so bright that he threw himself backwards, uttering a cry so savage that one might have thought that he had just seen some monstrous apparition in the divine armor.

"Deceived in his hope of vengeance, the unknown came back at a rapid pace toward the icy troop of the dead that he had just extracted from their long night; then, having contemplated them for some time with an infernal joy, he addressed himself to the dead man who had been covered by the nameless stone.

"'Well,' he said, 'have I not kept my promise, and has your insensate pride not received a punishment worthy of me? You thought to immortalize your name by associating it with the most splendid work to which the children of men had ever attached their gaze; you thought you could hide from me with impunity a thought that I once conceived for the glory of the One against whom I alone dared to struggle! And to obtain the renown that would have immortalized your name, you dared to contest in cunning with me, who has eternity to do evil and the somber solitudes of my realm to dream of it!

"'You thought that I would allow, at the price of a soul whose pride would one day subject it to me, the completion of a temple that would have rallied to Christ, my vanquisher, all future generations; a temple whose dazzling richness of detail, sublime harmony of grandeur and majesty, are not made to be understood by your wretched intelligences! Now see! For eight centuries, Christian Europe has striven in vain to seize the thought of my work, which *I alone* could conceive and *I alone* could complete.

"'And while your architects, miserable plagiarists, have remained exhausted and stupid before a creation that overwhelmed them, they have said that gold alone was lacking for them to finish the house of Jehovah! And Germany was moved, and even the Protestant princes have come to bring their stone to the edifice. Then the scholars and the architects arrived, each with his *original plan*, and confusion did not take long to intrude into your modern Babel; for the plan you possessed for an instant and for which, on the Eve of Christmas 1248, you renounced your God on the bank of the Rhine, that plan, here it is!'

"And the unknown took from his bosom a vast golden sheet on which the pale dead man saw, radiant in streaks of fire, a gigantic, superhuman edifice combining the most complete ideal of Christian thought and the richest liberty in form and variety.

"At that sight, the poor dead man began to sob, saying: 'Oh, an entire eternity of pain and torture in order that my name might be revealed to humans and fill the future!'

"'What are you complaining about?' said the unknown, with a bitter smile. 'Have you not had your name, your homeland and your age engraved on a bronze plaque destined to be sealed into the portal of this monument, in order that posterity would not be ignorant of that which concerns you, and would be able to occupy itself with you every day? Well, that bronze plaque, that glorious blazon, on which you were counting to ensure your immortality, has rested on your bosom in your tomb since the hour of your death, and it will remain there as one of your tortures until the end of time. Look!'

"He made a sign to one of the little black workmen who were crowded at the entrance to the choir. The latter leapt into the grave with the agility of a goblin and returned triumphantly, holding in his hand a bronze tablet on which a man's name, the name of a town and a date were radiant.

"At that sight, the specter uttered heart-rending cries; but the unknown, as impassive as the rocks of the Drachenfels, went on: 'You see, nothing was lacking your immortality but my will. Your tumulary stone, colossal testimony of your pride, your lie, was the last of your hopes. It sufficed for me to pass my hand over it to efface every last trace of your renown. Look!'

"The black workers turned over the sepulchral stone as if it were a light brick, and the sad specter saw with anguish that its surface was as smooth as if the chisel had never bitten into it.

"'And yet,' the unknown continued, 'while you were sleeping your long sleep of death, which, thanks to me, was not dreamless, scholars were searching for your name in order to crown it with an aureole of glory, and the noise of their footfalls awoke echoes in your coffin several times while they rummaged in the least corners of this edifice, in which they hoped one day to discover your name. Oh, you thought you could compete with me, with the one who fell under Jehovah's thunderbolts!'

"He began to laugh, with a laugh so strident and so terrible that all the dead men snatched from their cold dwellings trembled, shivering beneath their damp shrouds.

"'That isn't all, however,' the unknown went on. 'How could it serve me to have erased your name from the memory of the living as I have effaced it from that tumulary granite? It is necessary, *and I desire*, in order for my vengeance to be complete, that you and all those who have taken some part in the erection of this monument that I have condemned, you and all those who have thought yourselves able to vanquish my will in seeking to raise to the heavens these towers on which my malediction weighs, be condemned to undo every night the work that the living accomplish every day, until the grass has covered the last of these stones!'

"And, raising his formidable whip over the frightened crowd that surrounded him, he chased them before him, crying out in his terrible voice: *'To work! To work! The time has come!'*

"Then a strange and terrifying spectacle was seen. The dismal electors, the pale archbishops and the bronze colossus that reposed on the tomb of Konrad, the founder of the cathedral, emerged from the choir with a solemn and heavy tread, while behind them pressed the host of trembling specters trying to avoid the whip of the unknown, who was chasing them before him, repeating: *'To work! The time has come!'*

"Undulating at the entrance to the choir was the animated flood of little black men, brandishing their whips impatiently. When they arrived at the gate of the choir, the dead were handed saws, drills and levers, and they went on their way, impassive and mute, toward various parts of the edifice, each one followed by a cohort of little black men, who appeared to have the duty of serving them as manual laborers.

"The specter of the nameless tomb was sent toward the portal, the most beautiful part of the edifice, to accomplish his task of destruction there. Konrad von Hochstaden and the two brothers Anton and Adolf were directed to the summit of the northern tower, where their heavy footfalls were soon heard resonating in the stone spiral stairway. The electors of Bavaria and the host that the unknown had chased before him remained in the nave and the aisles. Soon, the master gave the signal to begin, and the work of destruction commenced.

"The black workers who had, until then, remained motionless along the sides of the church, the partitions of the vaults and the columns, became animated, as if by enchantment, and set about swarming like ants. Some, armed with long whips, pressed the poor dead in their sacrilegious toil, lashing their old bones pitilessly; the others presented them with tools and helped them to deface the stones, weaken the keystones of vaults, scratch the ribs, break the iron bars binding the high windows. Black mobs, crouching on the capitals of columns and the ogives of galleries scraped the beautiful efflorescences of stone born under the chisels of old German masters. Others threw dust over the woodwork that covered it with a terrible lava, under the effort of which the knottiest oak was consumed.

"A legion had fallen upon the windows and choir like a flock of bats, and was occupied in corroding the lead and iron of the stained glass. Others, finally, went up and down in the towers. All that labor was accomplished in the most solemn silence, and with the calm of a dream. The unknown, like a terrible master, strolled around the vast basilica, surveying the progress of his work, exciting the lukewarm, encouraging the most ardent with his gaze. Sometimes he disappeared momentarily under the obscure arch of the porch, and then the silence was interrupted by the dolorous moaning of the nameless specter, whom the master was doubtless forcing to accomplish some strange sacrilege. Then he went back up into the tower of the crane,[1] where the three archbishops were occupied in the horrible task of destroying all that had previously been done by their care.

"The choir had fallen back into darkness and resounded with sobs. From the height of their stone pedestals, the apostles raised their supplicant hands toward Christ to implore the vanquisher of Hell to extend his arm and expel all those monstrous profaners with a glance. Icy tears ran down their marble faces and fell on the flagstones like drops of molten lead.

"Suddenly, the twelve Christian peers quit their columns and surrounded their divine master, and a voice was heard saying: 'Do not permit, O Redeemer, these things to be accomplished! Expel with a breath all these children of darkness and protect your house against their sacrilegious enterprises!'

"But Christ remained mute on his cross and did not raise his head, lowered by the agony of Golgotha.

"Then, three strangers emerged from the depths of the choir, wearing vestments of silk and gold, like those

---

1 The fifteenth century crane left in place on the southern tower when work on the cathedral was suspended was still there in 1857, having long become an important symbolic landmark.

of princes and mages of the Orient. In their hands they held rich presents of myrrh, incense and pearls.

"They arrived at the foot of the cross, and said: 'O divine Savior, whom we had the glory of being the first to salute in your cradle, say a word in order to snatch your temple from the destruction that threatens it.'

"But Christ remained mute on his bloody wood and did not open his lips, frozen by the night of Golgotha.

"Then a woman, her head crowned with stars, whose calm and pure gaze seemed to reflect the heavens, descended from the column, bowed down before the cross and said with a sigh: 'My son, in the name of my superhuman dolor, of my heart lacerated by your sublime immolation, extend your hand and expel to their somber regions these accursed individuals who are soiling our temple and want to destroy it.'

"All remained mute, and Christ did not extend his sovereign hand, nailed to the bloody wood of Golgotha.

"At that sight, the apostles and the Magi, who had retained hope until then in the intervention of the Queen of Heaven, returned to their golden fames, weeping bitterly and saying: 'The time has come! The new law is accomplished and the temple is going to crumble. Woe unto us, who will no longer have such calm and silent retreats in which to praise the Lord!'

"The black companions of the unknown were still working, and his terrible spur was pressing the mute workers he had extracted from the tomb for this work of vengeance.

"Suddenly, a voice that appeared to emerge from the depths of the sanctuary let fall these words: 'When I was with you, when I was among the children of men, I said to them: *With faith you shall move mountains and you shall bid the angry waves of the sea to be calm.* Where faith is lacking, strength and the intelligence of divine things is lacking. The saints moved hills, but men can no longer move these stones; my spirit no longer animates them, for pride and egotism have replaced love!

"'What does it matter to my name whether this work is accomplished? Do I not have my temples in the solitudes of seas and on the slopes of mountains and glaciers? That is where my spirit dwells; that is where intelligence of my word will be obtained. It is to themselves and not to me that men have raised this monument. On the day when my father withdrew his hand from his people, the work of Solomon fell. On the day when Germany withdrew from me, it was struck with impotence; let it struggle with the enemy, then, in order that the new law shall also have its Babel, its trophy of the superb and of folly.'

"And the voice fell silent.

"Suddenly, a pale light illuminated the high windows; a ray of sunlight gilded the summit of the choir. At that sovereign light, the black swarm of infernal workers disappeared, as if by enchantment, and the cold statues and the dismal dead went to resume their beds of marble and earth.

"That is what Fritz the carpenter saw during the night he spent under the roof of the cathedral, and that is what he told me, swearing on his eternal salvation that he would not work on the dome any longer, even if they gave him ten thalers a day."

III

Franck had finished his story, but all the members of his audience were still listening. As the terrible drama of which Fritz had been the obligatory witness unfurled in their unquiet and curious minds, the attitude of the students had become increasingly grave. They had listened at first while smoking and making numerous visits to the vast bowl flaming before them; then, gradually, the pipes had been set down on the table or lined up along the wall; the glasses had remained empty, and a mute immobility had replaced the nervous agitation that troubles every auditor who is only listening out of politeness.

Of all the young men, however, the one who had extended all the force of his soul in order better to grasp the circumstances of the strange narrative was Ulric. For him, the impression had been sharper than for any other. His nature, attracted to marvelous things, had enabled him to see in his mind's eye the infernal vision that he almost regretted not having witnessed. That nameless specter, disappointed in his pride and glory, that mysterious unknown, hastening by blows of his terrible whip his work of destruction, and all the rest, had impressed him profoundly and awakened in him foolish, strange thoughts that he would not have dared to admit to his friends, but which took possession of his mind in solitude and hovered over his soul like black birds around a prey.

That inclination of the Germanic mind might seem strange to ordinary readers, who cannot fail to find it quite ridiculous that half a dozen German students could employ their leisure by occupying themselves with the Devil

30

and the part he plays in the things of this world. In a similar situation, French students would have passed the time talking about La Chaumière, the Dîner Millaud, the best method of cleaning pipes and the latest caricature in the *Charivari*; English students would have drunk ten bowls of punch earnestly, while proving that the Pope is the Antichrist and that Queen Victoria has the keys to paradise and parliament in her pocket; Flemish students would have emptied twenty tankards of beer without saying a word; but German students can only wander in the unknown spaces of the invisible world, and from there to the Devil it is only a single step.

Then too, Germany was always the hearth of somber legends of the spirit of evil, who manifests himself more readily in the Occident than in the luminous countries of the South. The North of Europe is full of traditions in which the cloven hoof of Satan shows itself, while the South seems reserved for Oriental superstitions, such as fays, djinn and the last guardians of treasures. We do not want to explain here the causes of that radical difference between the traditions of the North and the Orient of Europe; we shall limit ourselves to observing the fact. As for the authority of those traditions, let it suffice us to say that the best minds of the first Christian centuries and the highest intelligences of the fifteenth and sixteenth centuries never disputed the veracity of facts supported by witnesses as numerous as they were respectable.

"Your Fritz is a drunkard who must have been intoxicated," said Max, shaking himself, as if to rid himself of the impression produced on all his guests by that somber story. "And after getting drunk, he lay down on a bed of wood-chips, where he would have been subject to the obsession of all the horned reveries that accompany an indigestion of Bavarian beer. All the prodigies in the world have had for witnesses men who had silenced their reason in the depths of tankards."

"Fritz was so little intoxicated," said Franck, "that he had fasted since midday and had not drunk a glass beer or wine all day; and if you require a further proof of the terrible emotions that he experienced during that night of anguish, I'll tell you that he went into the cathedral with magnificent brown hair, which, at present, is mingled with as many gray hairs as the poor fellow could reasonably dread at the age of fifty."

"Max is a Voltairean," said Ulric, "who only adds his faith to material things, which means that he does not believe in galvanism, or electricity, or light, or inexplicable prodigies, but thinks magnetism undeniable—a man, in sum, who denies everything that cannot be measured by the geometer's compasses and is not manifest beneath the anatomist's scalpel. For myself, I think that your carpenter Fritz has had a stroke of luck that many people would envy him."

"Aha!" said Max, smiling. "Would you, by chance, have a desire to enjoy a private audience with His Tenebrous Majesty?"

"I don't say that," said Ulric, "but I would like to have seen that mysterious unknown, if only to assure myself as to whether Milton and Flaxman,[1] two men of genius, have been faithful in the descriptions they have left us of the beautiful fallen seraph. I've always detested the trivial manner in which Luther talked about Satan."

———————————

1 The second reference is presumably to John Flaxman's sculpture of "Saint Michael Overcoming Satan," exhibited in 1822.

"Friend," said Franck, gravely, "your words are foolish or dangerous, and woe betide you if they have passed through your heart before arriving at your lips."

Ulric lowered his head, as if his conscience had cast a secret reproach at him, but Max, still mocking, took up the conversation, which threatened to lapse.

"So," he said, "to summarize all of that, the Devil doesn't want Cologne cathedral to be finished, and in order to realize that idea, he employs the very individuals who once invested all their glory in endowing Germany with the most beautiful Christian temple ever risen from the earth toward God, like the prayer of a great people. Now we've reached the predicted time. The old dragon has broken his chain and reopened the pit of the abyss. He is coming to prowl the world again, sowing treasures and crowns. In truth, that will break the *monotony of the situation* somewhat, as the French put it."

"That Satan is distributing terrestrial wealth," said Ulric, "I can believe; but that he can give men things that take their source from God, such as talent or genius . . . that seems difficult to me."

"You're forgetting the specter of the nameless tomb," said Franck. "That man wanted glory, a name surrounded by an immortal aureole, but his work has remained truncated and incomplete, and his name will forever be a mystery for humans."

"Perhaps," Ulric observed, timidly, "he was unfaithful to a pact he made with the unknown, and without that disloyalty, who knows whether Germany might not count him among its most illustrious children, and whether the King of Bavaria might not have placed him in his Germanic Valhalla, between Albrecht Dürer and the great

Hermann, vanquisher of Varus."

"Which is to say," said Franck, "that you think that one can buy terrestrial glory at the price of one's soul and eternal reprobation."

"No," said Ulric, "but I believe that God has pardons for all human miseries, for all the weaknesses of the flesh, and I think that he ought to have extended his mercy to the man who was only criminal because he wanted to raise a temple worthy of his power."

"Say a temple to his impious pride," exclaimed Franck, "for if that sentiment had not animated him to the exception of any other; if he had understood that the works of men are only an inspiration from on high, his glory would have been pure and his name would be radiant in letters of gold on the parvis of the cathedral that weighs today upon the bosom of a damned soul!"

"Enough demonology for today, Messieurs," said Max, tapping the table with his pipe. "I declare the session ended, but I owe it to the truth to add that our friend Ulric manifests sympathies that do honor to his heart and his generosity. It is good to defend the old cloven hoof nowadays, when so many people do not even do him the honor of believing in his existence."

The students got up in order to return to their rooms. Ulric followed the general example, and a few minutes later he was sitting on his modest couchette, dreaming of the mysterious unknown, the Prince of Darkness summoning his subjects to a sacrilegious task and condemning his victims to efface every last trace of the glory to which they had sacrificed even the salvation of their souls.

Ulric's life in Heidelberg was that of every moderately conscientious student who does not accord the twenty-four hours of the day to fencing, the pipe, the tavern and gallant adventures. He followed a course in law assiduously, and spent his days doggedly scrutinizing the mysteries of the legislation of ancient peoples, Germanic customs and the law of the Empire. The evenings went by in philosophical conversations, which, by a strange fatality, always ended up turning to the most complete mysticism and taking literally the most apocalyptic pages of Swedenborg, the king of illuminates, whose writings have unhinged many a German mind.

In the midst of his studies, however, Ulric had not forgotten his love of poetry. He pored regretfully over digests and commentaries, and his thoughts wandered in the increate spaces of fantasy while his eyes remained mechanically fixed on the Pandects or the origins of Germanic law. Every day, his artistic nature awakened more energetic and vivacious, and his ambitious dreams went to nothing less than donning the crown that ornamented the head of Schiller or Goethe.

The German literary movement was particularly remarkable after the fall of Napoléon, who inspired so many admirable odes in the German muse, some of which respired all of the implacable Scandinavian ferocity. The voice of poets had given birth to battalions, and the grateful peoples regarded Körner and Max von Schenkendorf as men of election, invested with a national mission, whose songs caused all souls to quiver with a masculine enthusiasm. That glory, so great and so pure, had to be envied by Ulric, and his imagination was soon no longer dreaming of anything but one of those works that are the fleurons of the literary crown of a nation.

For a long time, Ulric had been working in silence on a great national epic that would reproduce in a dramatic manner the great struggles of the Empire under Frederick Barbarossa. Every day he walked alone beneath the great oaks that shade the ruins of the old castle of Heidelberg, meditating on his cherished work, the one from which he expected glory and fortune. Often, in the midst of his reveries, a herdsman, bringing back his sheep, stopped momentarily; then, having gazed at him for some time with the anxious curiosity of an illiterate peasant who sees a grimoire in all writing and cabalistic formulae in any printed paper, he withdrew, whistling at a large black dog which helped him to police his flock.

One day, when rebel inspiration refused to descend from its cloud to obey the voice that was invoking it, and the chagrined Ulric had just ripped up, ill-humoredly, a few pages whose fragments he cast to the winds, the herdsman approached him.

"My young lord," he said, saluting the young man respectfully, "others have tried before you to discover the place where the Golden Goat is hidden, but none have been able to reach it thus far. Some have employed an army of miners and have searched the ruins in every direction; others have read strange words in bulky books, but the earth keeps what has been confided to her."

"I don't know what treasure you're talking about, friend," Ulric said, smiling. "It's true that I'm seeking a treasure that will give me glory and wealth, if I'm fortunate enough to conquer it, but that one, it's not necessary to disinter with a pick-ax or magic words, because it's hidden here." He struck his forehead proudly as he spoke.

The herdsman looked at Ulric with a gaze in which, beneath an apparent stupidity, a profound suspicion glittered.

"You students, sire, like to mock poor peasants, for, if you don't know of the existence of the Golden Goat, why are you to be found every day sitting on the exact spot where it disappeared, leaving one of its horns in the hands of Doctor Faustus, who tried to seize it?"

"Oh!" said Ulric, impatiently. "What's this you're telling me about horns and Doctor Faustus' goat? I tell you again, friend, that the treasure I seek isn't guarded by dragons, like that of the Nibelungen."

"You're very fortunate to be able to read, to be a scholar," said the peasant, who seemed to be completing aloud a thought commenced internally. "If I knew how to read, I wouldn't he guarding dirty livestock; I'd have a schloss, dogs and woods in which to hunt roe dear and red deer."

"And you'd acquire all that if you knew how to read?" said Ulric, smiling. "In that case, why don't you go to a schoolmaster and study ardently?"

"Because it isn't certain that if I knew how to read a German book, I'd be able to understand the language in which the book is written that would render me master of the Golden Goat."

"What book?" asked Ulric, on whom the mysterious and convinced attitude of the herdsman was beginning to take effect.

The peasant darted a rapid glance around him to make sure that no one could hear him; then, approaching the young man, he took hold of his arm forcefully and said:

"You seem like an honest man; you wouldn't want to deceive a poor fellow who trusts your loyalty; very well, listen to me: three months ago, a stranger came to the ruins of the castle, accompanied by two domestics. The stranger wandered around the ruins for a long time, holding a book in his hand, which he set down from time to time, in order to look around. His domestics, in the meantime, kept watch to see whether anyone was coming. One of them stood on that section of wall you can see and cast a rapid glance over the surrounding area, and then, having made sure that it was deserted, went back to find his companion, who was already lying in the grass smoking his pipe."

"Well, what does all this have to do with the Golden Goat?" asked Ulric, impatiently.

"This, Sire: the following day and the days thereafter, the stranger came back on his own, sat down in the most deserted part of the ruins, and opened a book, from which he started to read, making grand gestures. At times he threw the book down, and then he spoke to the earth, the sky and the collapsed vaults, but nothing happened. Then he let his forehead fall into his hands and remained motionless, deep in thought."

"Where were you during this time, to see all that?"

"In the turret over there, the stairway of which is broken, and where no one but me dares to risk himself," said the peasant, with a proud smile. "Now, a week ago, the stranger came back to take his accustomed place at the entrance to the crypts of the chapel. That place is one of the most dangerous in the ruins, for the vault of the choir, in the part that touches the nave, has a crack more than fifty feet long, through which you can see the sky. The rest of the vault is covered by a veritable forest of fir-trees, whose roots have traversed the stones, without which it would have caved in.

"So, the stranger sat down on the capital of a column and began to read his old book, as usual. But all of a sudden, the sky darkened; a horrible tempest whistled though the ruins and bent the fir-trees that were growing over the

vault of the chapel. The turret I was in seemed to be moving under the redoubled gusts of wind. From where I was,
I could see the stranger through the breach in the vault of
the choir, walking back and forth reading aloud from his
book, without paying any heed to the whirlwind that was
pounding the trees over his head. For a moment, the wind
seemed to die down, but suddenly it resumed with such a
fury that one might have thought that the air was full of
roaring demons. Stones fell, as thick as hail, the firs broke
with terrible cracking sounds, and the hurricane carried
the branches away through the ruins.

"Suddenly, a muffled noise rose above that of the tempest; one might have thought it the explosion of a mine.
I looked, fearfully: it was the vault of the chapel that had
just collapsed. In the midst of a vast heap of stones that
filled the void between the walls, a few tops of broken
fir-trees could be seen sticking out, and, buried under a
mountain of rubble, which must also have covered the
body of the unfortunate stranger. . . ."

"Doubtless," said Ulric, "you made haste to bring help
to the poor man?"

"I'm not one of those who want to joust with Satan,"
said the peasant. "I understood that the man had been
the victim of his ignorance in magic, that he had made a
mistake in his incantation, and that the Devil had crushed
him under the debris of the vault. As no one had witnessed the scene, I thought that I might become rich and
happy if I could procure the stranger's book. The crypt in
front of which the stranger had been sitting had another
entrance; I slipped into it, and at the door that opened into
the choir, I saw a hand sticking out from beneath a heap
of bloody stones, which was holding a book. I made the

sign of the cross and prized it out of the fingers that were gripping it. Then I covered that black hand, which scared me, with stones, and I took the book home."

There was enough in the peasant's narrative to excite an interest in a nature less devoted to the marvelous than Ulric's. The tempest, the stranger crushed beneath the ruins of a chapel, and the mysterious book all stirred the young man's imagination forcefully.

"And what does the book contain?" he said to the peasant, "for you to have had the courage to go and obtain it, at the price of a sacrilege, by snatching it from the hand of a cadaver?"

"I'm not so stupid," said the herdsman, with an expression pierced by the instinctive suspicion that replaces the enlightenment of education in the agricultural classes, "as to go and show it to just anyone, who would find therein the means of removing the treasure hidden in the ruins and say to me afterwards: 'My dear Wilhelm, your book is a book like any other, and there's no more a treasure in the ruins of Heidelberg than in the cupboard of the village schoolmaster.'" The herdsman became animated. "No, I want to be rich, to have woods in which to hunt roe deer without fear of gamekeepers. I want to be rich, to render to my master all the scorn he's lavished on me, and all the insults to which he's subjected me since I've been looking after these accursed beasts, which graze here in peace all day long and grow fat visibly, while hunger sticks my skin to my bones and hatred puts an inferno in my heart."

As he spoke thus, the herdsman's gaze shone with a somber fire; by means of his iron-tipped staff he broke, angrily, the sweet-briars and wild mulberries that grew in the midst of the ruins. After a silence of a few minutes, he raised his head again, looking at Ulric, and said to him in the humble and coaxing voice of a man who senses his weakness and understands that he can do nothing without the help of another:

"Look, my young master, I don't know what pushed me toward you and why you inspire the confidence in me that urges me to reveal a secret to you on which my fortune depends—and yours, if you want to help me—but your sad and gentle face has impressed me, and seeing you come here every day and speak aloud, I've understood that, like me, you have reason to lament your fortune; that like me, you're seeking the treasure of the Golden Goat, but that you lack the veritable book by the sole means of which one can bring it out of the secret crypt in which it's contained. Now, swear to me on your baptism to share the treasure honestly with me, and not to seek to abuse my ignorance, and I'll go fetch the book for you this instant."

"My friend," said Ulric, keenly intrigued by the shepherd's air of conviction, "you have a poor sick mind and your heart is nourishing evil thoughts. This book, which, according to you, might put you in possession of a treasure, is surely nothing but an ordinary book, or a tissue of sacrilegious fables by means of which impious men hope to invoke the spirits of the abyss. Go fetch me the book, and I promise you that if it should reveal a treasure, to share it with you as an honest German."

"Really?" said Wilhelm, dubiously.

"I swear it," said Ulric, in a grave voice.

"Follow me, then," said the herdsman. "I'm only a rustic, the least of herdsmen, but if you ever deceive me, I'd be able to avenge myself, even if you were a Palatine Count of the Empire."

IV

Wilhelm, having said a few words to his dog, set off in the direction of the collapsed chapel. The debris of the vault of the principal nave obstructed the doorway and prevented entry to the aisles that were still intact. On the heels of his companion, Ulric climbed over the ruins, from the middle of which the tops of fir-trees occasionally protruded. Having arrived at the summit of the rubble, they descended again into one of the lateral naves, half filled-in by debris, and the shepherd opened a door that gave access to a cloister paved with tumulary stones hidden in long grass.

By means of his iron-tipped staff, he lifted the slab of a tomb, and, plunging his arm into the interior, drew out a book, which, to judge by its external appearance, as well as the form of the binding, did not seem to date back more than a few years.

"Give me the book," said Ulric. "I'll tell you in an instant on what your hopes of ambition and fortune rest."

"Not here! Not here!" said Wilhelm, in a mysterious and muted voice. "That might bring us bad luck. And then, it's necessary not to read the book without preparation, or at hazard. It's that ignorance of the rules, it's necessary to observe, that impelled the demons to crush the stranger under the ruins of the chapel."

Ulric was subject, without suspecting it, to the influence of his companion's profound faith in the power of the mysterious book. Then too, the closer, the ruins, and the manuscript confided to the sepulcher, after being torn from the hand of a cadaver, were all circumstances that acted, if not on his intelligence, at least on his nerves. He therefore followed his guide, and they both soon arrived outside the porch of the chapel, around which Wilhelm's flock was peacefully grazing under the guard of the black dog.

The sun was about to set, and illuminated the high walls of the chapel with a bloody glow. On their summit, rooks and crows seemed to be conversing in raucous voices. Ulric sat down on a stone, and took the book from Wilhelm's hands. Before entrusting the precious treasure to him, the latter reminded him of his oath, which the young man, devoured by impatience and curiosity, ratified again with solemn words.

Wilhelm sat down opposite Ulric, in such a fashion as to be able to interrogate with his gaze all the modifications of the young man's face and scrutinize his most secret thoughts. Still suspicious, he feared, in spite of Ulric's oath, that the latter might seek to deceive him as to the importance of the mysterious book. He was, in consequence, sitting there, his eyes riveted to his companion's face, cursing the ignorance that forced him to admit a stranger to a division for which he had committed a kind of sacrilege.

Ulric opened the book with a sort of dread and darted a rapid glance at the title. It was a manuscript in beautiful German handwriting, which appeared to date from the seventeenth century.

The first page bore for a title:

THE TREASURE OF THE NIBELUNGEN
A Collection of Germanic traditions gathered for the first time in the form of a dramatic trilogy by . . .[1]

---

1 It is, of course, highly unlikely that Richard Wagner made a pact with the Devil in order to produce the Ring cycle in the 1870s, but his epic cycle of operas recycling the legends of the Nibelungenlied was

A large bloodstain, mingled with dust and chalk, rendered the name of the author illegible.

Ulric scanned the mysterious manuscript rapidly, in which he saw united for the first time, in a dramatic form, the admirable fragments that Germany possesses of its old heroic songs. His gaze scanned the pages, in which a style as virile and proud as that of Schiller, and as pure and limpid as that of Goethe, was combined with the most expert dramatic contexture. Although initiated into all the beauties of German literature, Ulric could not help uttering a cry of admiration on reading that work, in which all the harsh and proud genius of the North was reflected, embellished and heightened by all the prestige of the most savant and ingenious art.

Ulric's exclamation had not escaped Wilhelm. He drew nearer to his companion abruptly, interrogating him with his gaze.

"Oh!" cried Ulric, electrified by the beauty of a poem whose existence no one in Germany suspected. "This is a book in which every page is the fleuron of an immortal crown, a magic talisman whose words enchain fortune and glory to the footsteps of its fortunate possessor!"

Wilhelm, his eyes ablaze and his bosom panting, devoured the young man's words. The latter seemed to have forgotten the presence of his companion, and was riffling through the manuscript posed on his knees with a kind of fever.

"Well," said Wilhelm, "you can see that I didn't deceive you when I told you that book would make us rich enough to buy a principality, or at least a duchy. To think that each

undoubtedly a response to the same crucial Romantic magnetism that is here drawing Ulric into its power.

word of that volume is going to render us masters of all the joys of the earth! Hurrah for the Golden Goat! If it showed itself at this moment I'd kiss its hoof, even if it were cloven like Satan's. Away with filthy cows and miry pigs, and long live gold and good cheer!"

These words, inspired by a coarse and sensual thought, caused Ulric to fall from the lofty regions where his mind was soaring. His enthusiasm was chilled by contact with that rapacious cupidity, which thought of nothing but gold and saw nothing beyond terrestrial lusts.

Then a strange thought appeared in the depths of his soul. What was to prevent him from extracting a few fragments from that poem, which no one knew, and whose author lay buried under a mountain of ruins, initially under an assumed name, in order to test public curiosity and acquire the conviction that no one in the world except him suspected its existence?

And if that were the case, said the serpent of pride that was already raising its crest in one of the darkest recesses of his heart, what was to prevent him from attaching his name to the work, and taking his place at a single bound in the sublime heights where Homer, Shakespeare, Dante and Schiller were seated?

That thought had traversed Ulric's mind like a flash of lightning, and while his companion delivered himself to the impulses of his brutal joy, he was already reproaching his poetic enthusiasm, in which Wilhelm could not fail to see anything but the intoxication of cupidity and the wild joy of a man to whom hazard has just given the key that opens the doors of all terrestrial Edens.

It was, therefore, with an embarrassed expression and an ill-assured gaze that Ulric replied to his companion.

"I'm sorry to disabuse you, my poor Wilhelm, but this isn't what you think. There's no question in this book either of treasure, an enchanted goat, or riches with which to buy a duchy. It's a collection of old German songs, and . . ."

"Your voice tells me that you're lying," said Wilhelm, angrily, "and you want to keep the treasure for yourself—but by the Devil, it won't be thus! Old songs! Do you take me for a fool, then, to tell me such tales? Give me the book and I'll find, God willing, more honest men than you, who'll be only too happy to share with me a fortune that will permit them to have vines on the mountain and manors in the valley!"

"Gently, friend," said Ulric, tranquilly pushing away the herdsman's hand. "This book is certainly very precious, but not in the sense that you lend it, at least. There's no question of treasure, I assure you."

"Really!" said Wilhelm, sarcastically. "But if that's the case, why, after scarcely having glanced at it, did you cry out like a madman that every page was the fleuron of a crown, of which the book was a magic talisman that would give fortune and glory to its possessor? Have you, then, forgotten your own words, master?" The shepherd struck his forehead. "As for me, they're still there! In any case, I repeat, give the book back to me. Others than you will tell me what remains for me to do."

Ulric judged his situation at a glance; to destroy the impression that his enthusiastic speech had made on the shepherd's mind was impossible and dangerous. The other's belief in the mysterious power of the manuscript that Ulric held, and the existence of a treasure, was like one of those stakes profoundly driven into the ground that one embeds more solidly in trying to loosen them. On the other hand, to return to Wilhelm the poem on which his thought had just built, in a moment, an entire future of fortune and glory, was to renounce foolishly one of the rare favors that fortune keeps for her favorites; it was to make known the existence of a literary treasure that no one suspected, and which he could appropriate without danger. And yet, it was necessary at all costs, to keep it and hide it from all gazes!

But Wilhelm was there, as rapacious and menacing as a wolf lying in wait for a prey, and, with his arm extended toward Ulric, he was waiting for the latter to hand him back the talisman that was to awaken the magic goat from her age-old sleep and make her deliver the gold confided to her care.

A black and sinister thought crossed the young man's mind. What if the herdsman, in spite of his words and pleas, were to persist in his determination—if his blind cupidity led him to deliver to the examination of a third party those heroic songs that a secret voice told him were to be known to him alone? Then, adieu his dreams of glory and ambition, and all the magical enchantments evoked by his delirious pride!

It was, therefore, with a chagrin ill-disguised under the appearances of a false bonhomie that Ulric replied to the shepherd, who, his eyes full of suspicion, was awaiting his response while clutching his iron-tipped staff in his right hand.

"You're mistaken as to the meaning of my words, my dear Wilhelm; you've misinterpreted my enthusiasm. Certainly, in my hands this book might have some value, but in yours it would be scarcely more precious than the dead leaves beneath our feet."

"And why is that?" said the shepherd. "Because you know how to read it? Well then, say the words! The sun hasn't set yet and one can see well enough to distinguish a pot of gold from a heap of rubble."

"You don't see anything in the world more precious than gold, then?" said Ulric, with a disdainful irony that could not help but pierce the coarse envelope of the herdsman.

"Well," said Wilhelm, with a noisy laugh, "what can you see, then, that's more precious? With gold I'd have land, houses, fine clothes, and my comrades today would take off their hats when I passed before them, preceded by a hunter emplumed like the Graf von Rheinstein's. Find me many things then, that have that power to make a dirty herdsman like me a great lord, at whom beautiful ladies wouldn't disdain to smile!"

"However, admitting for a moment," said Ulric, who wanted to interrogate one of the more sensitive cords of the mind of the German peasant, "that the book has the virtue you suppose, how do you know that the treasure wouldn't cost you your repose in this world and your salvation in the other?"

The herdsman remained thoughtful for a moment, and appeared to be interrogating himself.

"Remember," said Ulric, gravely, "that treasures confided to the earth are guarded by evil spirits, and that the demon is no less the demon for appearing to you in the form of a goat, even one of gold."

"Say the words boldly!" said Wilhelm, raising his head confidently. "I have no fear! I have a blessed cross that has touched the bones of the three Kings of Cologne. Then again, I'm baptized, and the Devil can't do anything to those who have faith in their baptism, according to our parish priest. And after all, when I'm rich, I'll be able to build a chapel to Saint Hermann, and have masses said for the remedy of my soul. Say the words, master—and hurry up, for the sun is already sinking behind that hill over there, and the bats of the ruins are already commencing to flutter around us."

The stupid obstinacy of the herdsman, always harking back to his favorite theme, irritated Ulric. He suffered in his pride and his vanity in seeing the angular stone of his future delivered to the mercy of a cupid individual whose blind superstition saw nothing in the manuscript but a talisman containing magic words by means of which the earth would open and render the treasures confided to infernal gnomes. Then too, he sensed vaguely that Wilhelm was a dangerous witness to the deceptive endeavor that he was about to undertake—and a witness in such a circumstance was an enemy, a single word from whom could topple the entire edifice of his future renown.

"You're a madman, whose head has been turned by ambition and avarice," said Ulric, bitterly. "This book is not a book of magic, and I could read it to you from now until tomorrow without a single kreutzer or pfennig falling upon you from the sky."

"Since that's the case," said the shepherd, "give it back to me. I know what I know, me! And it was very good of me to admit you to a share of something to which you have no right. So, give the book back to me, and be off with you!"

"Look," said Ulric, "you're a poor sick brain with which it's impossible to reason. But as it's just that you obtain a price for your find, here's a gold frederick for your book, which certainly isn't worth a thaler."

"Really?" said the shepherd, sniggering. "You'll pay a gold frederick for something that isn't worth a thaler, and that to a man you don't know? And you think I'm stupid enough not to see all the crudity of your knavery! By the Devil! I thought the doctors of the university less maladroit. Now, I ask you for the last time, give that book back to me. There's already blood on one of its pages—be careful there isn't also yours."

And, matching action to words, Wilhelm advanced, brandishing his iron-tipped staff, a terrible weapon of which a single blow might be mortal. On seeing the herdsman marching toward him with that insulting attitude, Ulric's patrician blood was inflamed. His nostrils quivered and his eyes gleamed. He darted a rapid glace around him, as if to study the battlefield.

Behind him were the ruins of the chapel. Wilhelm, on the other hand, had his back to the broken ramparts of the castle, which, built on the bare rock, rose up more than a hundred and fifty feet above the valley. No vestige of wall remained at that point, one of the most dangerous in the ruins, while behind Ulric, the residue of the rampart rose up three or four feet from the ground.

The young man retreated a few steps, clutching the manuscript in one hand like a shield, while is right hand searched in his pocket for one of those strong Solingen daggers, the *vade mecum* of German students: an innocent weapon, to be sure, which was only bloodied once, in the breast of Kotzebue.[1]

---

1 The German dramatist August von Kotzebue (1761-1819), a significant figure in the Romantic Movement, was murdered by a member

The shepherd roared with fury on seeing the murderous blade in the young man's hand.

"Oh! You want to murder me in order better to rob me afterwards! But by the Devil, you aren't where you think with me, and your piece of iron doesn't scare me."

As he finished speaking, Wilhelm launched a terrible blow of his stick at the young man, who avoided it by leaping sideways. The staff, falling in the wrong place, broke on the crumbled stones. Drunk with rage, the peasant hurled himself at Ulric in order to stun him with the stump that he still had in his hand, but at that moment his foot slipped on the debris. He seized Ulric by the throat in order to maintain himself, and dragged him down with him as he fell. There was a desperate struggle for a moment, grim and pitiless, the herdsman trying to strangle the young man with his callused hands, and the latter trying to escape from his enemy's mortal embrace.

Finally, sensing the impotence of his efforts and choking in the animate vice that was squeezing his throat, Ulric, impelled by an instinctive sentiment of self-preservation, plunged his dagger to the hilt in his enemy's heart.

The latter uttered a profound groan, his hands opened, and he rolled on the grass beside the semi-conscious Ulric.

During the time that the struggle had lasted, the sun had set and the shadows of evening had descended over the ruins. The fresh night air reanimated the young man and rendered him, along with the sentiment of his existence, the memory of the frightful struggle from which he had just emerged victorious.

---

of a student fraternity, who considered him to be an enemy of the people. Such fraternities were then abolished by the Carlsbad Decrees of 1819, which restricted academic freedom in Germany for some time.

He got up, as if moved by a spring, and saw with horror the inanimate body of Wilhelm lying on the grass. The moon, momentarily veiled by rain-bearing clouds, disengaged its brilliant crescent at that moment, and Ulric saw with fright that his hands were red with blood. At his feet was the fatal book over which two cadavers had already rolled, and whose pages had doubtless just been stained with blood for the second time.

Ulric's head was seething under a torrent of feverish thoughts. He sought to doubt the reality of his existence and the bloody deed with which he had just soiled himself. He bent down to look at the pale face of the shepherd, but he only saw a spectacle even more horrible than death—which is to say, hatred in death, the grim and petrified hatred surviving all sentiment and appearing only to be awaiting the trumpet of the angel to awaken again, implacable and thirsty for vengeance.

Rapidly, Ulric picked up the fatal manuscript and fled the ruins with his baleful trophy. He ran all the way down the steep path that led to the valley, not daring to look behind him, for fear of seeing a menacing and livid figure on his heels. Having arrived in the valley, he washed his hands in a stream, readjusted the order of his clothing, and took the road to the town.

Ten o'clock was chiming in all the bell-towers when he reached the threshold of his dwelling. He went up the stairs that led to his room at a mute and rapid pace, and, opening the door precipitately, threw himself down on the bed, exhausted and worn out, but still having before his eyes the implacable figure of Wilhelm lying in the briars, his face turned to the sky, as if to take it as his witness against his murderer.

V

It is a singular and inexplicable thing, the brilliant or somber veil that various states of mind cast over the objects that surround us. Ulric's little room, so pleasant and cheerful the day before, seemed to have put on the mourning of his soul. Remorse was seated at his hearth like an implacable and mute guest. All the thousand trivia forming as many bonds of intimate life and which seem to take on a friendly voice in the silence of meditation or study—his arms, his furniture, his pipes, his books—now seemed to be contemplating him with terror. The silence itself had a voice; the shadows were populated with menacing forms.

Ulric felt the need to extract himself from the torture of his thought. Franck and Max were not yet in bed, and the sonorous voice of the latter could be heard singing a verse from an old German song:

> *When you see my love, tell her that I salute her.*
> *If she asks how I am, tell her I'm on my feet.*
> *If she asks about my health, tell her that I'm dead.*
> *If the beauty starts to cry, tell her I'll see her tomorrow.*

Ulric sought to put on a countenance in harmony with the mental disposition that seemed to be animating his friends, and went in.

"Here's our poet," said Max, extending a benevolent hand to Ulric. "Do you know, gentlemen, that if we had a little heart, the laborious and calm existence of our friend would be a living remorse for us. While we smoke like freebooters and drink like sponges, and our principal occupation is wandering the streets like dog-catchers, our friend Ulric is reading, meditating, working, interrogating the dusty chronicles of old Germany and elevating in his thought one of those works that will permit a man to say: 'Now God can call me to him, because I've lived!'

"On the contrary, what are we doing? We're foolishly wasting our intelligence and our youth on trivia: women, duels and pipes. We know where to find the best beer in Bavaria, which merchant sells the best cigars, and which is the tailor who possesses the most elegant cut; in brief, we live like soldiers of fortune, with no intelligence of the future, who imagine that God has put them on the earth to drink, smoke, make love and break glasses!"

Max threw his pipe on to the table, ill-humoredly. "Well, Ulric, if I didn't love you as I love you, I'd detest you as a living contrast, who renders more poignant the senti- ment of my intellectual and moral infirmities. Gentlemen, I propose a toast to our friend, and his future triumphs!"

And the large Bohemian cup made a tour of the circle, while Ulric, shaking Max's loyal hand, wondered silently whether he ought to reveal his adventure of the evening to that noble heart, or keep to himself, with the secret of that bloody action, that of the mysterious manuscript that he had acquired at the price of a murder, and which he did not dare open now, as if he might have read in its bloody pages the sentence that was murmuring dully in his conscience.

"Well, dreamer," Max said to Ulric, while the latter con- templated with a sentiment of envy and regret the pro- found calm and mild security that animated the faces of his friends, "are you making progress with your work, and will we soon be able to discrown that old pagan Goethe in order to circle your victorious head?"

"The times are propitious for poets," said Franck, in a grave tone. "In our day, Tasso would have made Leonora d'Este wait in his antechamber. People have finally understood the royalty of intelligence, and they salute in their poets the veritable anointed of the Lord, while we know what people think of damnable royalties on the boundary-markers of crossroads."

"Let our Ulric go his own way," said Max. "One of these days he'll reveal himself in a clap of thunder that will precipitate the Olympian Jupiter of Weimar from his throne of myths and symbols."

Those words, emerging from friendly mouths, went to reawaken the viper of pride, momentarily fallen sleep in Ulric's soul. The glory of which he had dreamed depended on him alone now. The poet's crown for which he was ambitious was there, ready-woven, and he alone could see the homicidal stain that tarnished its gleam. He passed his hand over his forehead, as if to chase away an important idea, and addressing his friends, asked them what they thought about a vast dramatic trilogy of which the subject would be borrowed from the Nibelungenlied.

"I think," said Franck, "that the idea alone is one of those inspirations that the muse only accords to her elect. And if you're able in your work to conserve the savage grandeur, the rude and proud poetry of those songs, while imprinting them with a beautiful dramatic development, I'll bow down before your genius, and Germany will salute in you the Homer of the Germanic epic."

"Well, brothers," said Ulric, "if you want to gather our common friends in a few days, I'll have the pleasure of reading you a few fragments of a work . . ."

"Which must have given you more than one headache, my poor friend," said Max, effusively. "You see, I only know the dolors of poetic gestation by hearsay, for God forgive me if I've ever done violence to those prudes the Muses other than by snatching from them a few wretched songs in which I made *wine* rhyme with *Rhine*."

"Why don't you read us something this evening?" said Franck. "The room is well-shuttered, the wind's howling outside, we're all in the most benevolent disposition, ready to hear you, to advise you, or to applaud you, in accordance with opportunity."

"Well spoken!" Max exclaimed. "And in order not to disturb you, tell me where you've put your manuscript. In three bounds, I'm in your room; with one leap, I'm back."

At this proposal, Max felt all his blood flow back toward his heard. Pale and trembling, he launched himself in font of his friend, stammering in a voice strangled by terror:

"No! Not this evening, not this evening, brother! I need to look again at what I want to read, and then, I'm tired, even ill, and feel the need to rest."

"Indeed," said Franck, your face is pale and distressed; your eyes are shining as if you had a fever. You've worn the poetic harness too long today, my poor troubadour; go to bed, and you can read your work to us tomorrow."

Ulric breathed in profoundly on seeing his friends renounce their project more easily than he had initially hoped. An imprudent circumstance might reveal his secret and compromise both his safety and his future. He retired, therefore, not without thinking, with terror, that he was about to find himself face to face with the bloody witness whose presence he had fled, and toward which a strange fatality was drawing him.

Having arrived in his room, Ulric made sure that no indiscreet gaze could reach him; then, having thrown himself on his bed, he began to reflect on his situation.

The thirst for renown had driven him to a culpable action, which his reason tried to justify by seeing it merely as a consequence of the instinct of self-preservation. And now vanity had just rendered any return toward the truth impossible. In confiding to his friends the existence of a work on which he was founding his future, he had riveted himself to his lie by an indestructible chain. To recoil was hazardous, and his serpent murmured in his ear that the noise of his glory would soon stifle the importunate and annoying voice that troubled his thoughts. And then, no witness could accuse him, unless the dagger found a voice or the crows of the ruins came to testify against him. He armed himself with an energetic resolution, and decided that he would publish a first fragment of the dramatic trilogy of the Nibelungen the following day, under an assumed name, in order to test the public and discover whether there was anyone else who had any knowledge of the existence of the mysterious manuscript.

Having taken that determination, he felt stronger; his blood was circulating more freely. He went to pick up the book tranquilly, and started to examine it with the cold curiosity of a bibliophile.

The entire work was written in a firm and clear hand. The title of the book indicated that no other copy existed. The name of the author had vanished, as we have said, under a large bloodstain.

Ulric set to work and spent a part of the night copying extracts from the manuscript, not without pausing from time to time, as if dazzled by the sublime beauties of the poem, compared with which Byron and Schiller paled. Sometimes, he stopped in order to read aloud what he had just written, but then his voice caused him a strange and indefinable impression of terror . . . and mocking murmurs seemed to circulate around him.

He worked until dawn blanched the sky; then, exhausted by the emotions of the day and the labors of the night, he threw himself on to his bed fully dressed, where he soon fell into a heavy and profound slumber.

The first fragment that was published in Germany of the dramatic trilogy of the Nibelungen produced a profound sensation. Everyone wondered anxiously who the original and bold poet might be who was hiding under a pseudonym, when it would have been sufficient to name himself to be saluted by the acclamations of the crowd. Apart from Franck and Max, Ulric's two friends, no one knew to whom to attribute the strange work that exhaled, like a savage perfume, the heroic barbarity of primitive Germany, and whose supple and vigorous style, ever colorful, took aboard all forms.

Franck, in whom his friend's work had inspired an admiration and a profound respect, begged Ulric every day to free him from his oath and allow him to be one of the heralds of his young renown, but Ulric had his reasons for continuing to retain an anonymity under which he wanted to acquire the conviction that no one but him knew the mysterious poem; and what his friends criticized as the consequence of an excessive modesty, was in him only the cold calculation of a vanity trembling to find itself unmasked one day.

Finally, when Ulric judged that nothing could any longer oppose the complete realization of his designs, when he saw all intelligences stirred and in quest of the mysterious poet who seemed disdainful of so many homages and enveloped himself in shadow when another would have demanded the thousand torches of publicity, he confided to Franck and Max his project of bringing together at a soirée the literary lions and the aristocracy of Heidelberg and neighboring cities, in order to submit to a kind of public proof the entire poem, mere fragments of which had so sharply pricked the curiosity of everyone, and of which everyone wanted to know the author.

Franck and Max, to whom Ulric had handed over the care of everything concerning that memorable solemnity, in which he wanted to reveal to Germany the unknown poet whose name was on all lips, were soon overwhelmed with requests and supplications of every kind. Young women and men recommendable as much by character as by talent, solicited as a signal favor the opportunity to salute the first new star that had risen on the splendid horizon of German art, where Goethe's star was already fading.

In the midst of all the commotion of which he was the object, Ulric waited with horrible heartbeats for the fatal moment when he would tear away the veil that had protected him thus far.

Sometimes, his reverie conducted him by flowery paths to a brilliant future, embellished by the acclamations and admiration of an entire people; he saw himself, the poor student lost in the crowd, receiving the homages of kings, and proudly wearing the simple crown of laurels with which nations are so miserly. Then, after those radiant hopes, everything darkened in his soul. He wondered whether some enemy might have the secret of his crime and his fraud, and was only waiting for the last moment to unmask him. Mortal frissons gripped him then like cold reptiles, and he wanted to die, cursing the day when he had opened his soul to his first dreams of ambition.

Thanks to the cares of Franck and Max, an elite gathering was to be present at the soirée that was preoccupying all of Germany. Around him, Ulric heard nothing but talk of the mysterious author of the trilogy of the Nibelungen, and no one suspected that the young blond head sunken beneath the invisible hand of remorse was the one for which so many crowns were being woven. Sometimes, as if terrified by the triumph that awaited him, he thought of running away and going to hide the tortures of his heart in the depths of Franconia; but then a secret influence seemed to hold him back, and a voice as soft as that of the fays that summon travelers to their homicidal dances in the evening murmured words of hope in his ear—magic words—and the young man's forehead rose up audacious and proud, as if he were preparing to do battle with misfortune.

Finally, the day so redoubted by Ulric and so desired by the crowd arrived. Baron von Reichmann, one of the most ardent admirers of the anonymous author of the Nibelungen, had consented to offer his reception rooms for the gathering. Franck was to introduce the unknown poet, for whom a private room had been prepared in the house. A young artiste known for several original sympathies had chosen the soirée to reveal to the public a new work.

Ulric, wrapped in a cloak that covered his face, had been introduced by Franck into a room which the latter locked with a key, until the moment when he had to come to collect his friend in order to introduce him to the acclamations of an impatient crowd and the gaze of so many young women, not one of whom would have been glad to shelter her amour from that radiant and nascent renown.

The room in which Franck had just locked his friend was a large one, hung with crimson lampas and ornamented with mirrors, some of which reflected one another. On entering that room, Ulric had thrown his cloak on to a table and leaned on the chimney-breast, allowing his mind to ride at hazard through all the foolish fantasies that pass through a mind whipped by fever. A single lamp played on the mantelpiece illuminated the room feebly, leaving large masses of shadow in the corners. In front of him, through the thick curtains, he could see the faint silhouettes of the guests, who seemed to be agitating impatiently, passing confusedly through the drawing-rooms opposite.

A distant sound of instruments reached his ears, but with the mysterious character that the songs have that we hear in our dreams; then his thoughts, simultaneously embracing the past, the present and the future, represented to him in a sequence of fugitive and mobile tableaux, all the phases of his life. He saw himself as a young man dreaming under the oaks of paternal forests; then as a poet with his forehead crowned with a crimson hood, figuring in the Germanic Valhalla. Sometimes, but like a rapid vision, he perceived the ruins of Heidelberg Castle, the collapsed chapel, the black and bruised hand holding the mysterious manuscript . . . and then the herdsman lying, all bloody in the moonlight that illuminated the menacing cadaver, whose lips seemed to have conserved the name of his murderer.

An indefinable malaise weighed simultaneously upon his soul and his body, and he was raising his head in order to go to open a widow overlooking the courtyard, when he perceived, standing at the other corner of the chimney-breast, with his head in his hand, an unknown man whose gaze was fixed upon him, with a strange smile.

The room in which Ulric was enclosed had only one door, the one that Franck had carefully locked, and the key to which he had taken away. No one, therefore, could have entered the room—and yet there, only separated from him by the width of the fireplace, was a man standing silently, whose footfalls had not troubled his reverie and whose fixed, implacable and profound gaze chilled Ulric to the very sources of life.

The unknown was dressed in a black velvet doublet, and a cap similar to that of German student was gracefully tilted over his ear. A superior intelligence radiated from his entire face, endowed with a beauty for which humans have no expression. Sometimes, his somber gaze seemed to be disarmed, and to sink into a limitless reverie—but a moment later, the ardent spark that sharpened his pupils reappeared, and with it, all the terrors of which the man seemed to be the king.

"You weren't expecting me?" said the unknown to Ulric, who was frozen with terror.

An inarticulate murmur was all that the young man's lips could proffer.

The unknown continued, in a grave but ironic tone; "Do you know that your audacity is at least equal to your ambitious folly? What—you want to conquer glory and fortune in a single day, without going to any other trouble than arming your face with impudence and representing the blush of your shame for that of modesty, the trouble of your conscience for the embarrassment of a debutant breaking his first lance? You march toward renown, trampling a cadaver underfoot; you collect your first palm with the aid of a dagger; you accumulate in one day murder, theft and fraud, and you say that you're not expecting me?"

And the unknown began to smile, while the terrified Ulric did not know whether or not he was under the obsession of a dream.

"Come on," sad the unknown, "time's pressing." He pointed at the resplendent reception rooms where the crowd was agitating. "There are three hundred people there, impatient to see you . . . young women ornamented with flowers, beauties to make one forget God, waiting, breasts palpitating, for the moment when you will deign to emerge from your cloud. Now, what name is it necessary to throw to that crowd . . . yours or mine?"

"Yours," said Ulric, with an astonishment mingled with fear. "But first of all, who are you?"

"One of the authors of that poem," said the unknown, disdainfully, pointing at the book placed on the table. "A modest author, sated by glory and the banal incense of human beings, who will gladly cede you his share of renown, for fear that his name might eclipse yours if it appears on a poster."

"And what tells me that you're not an impostor?" said Ulric, who had recovered his audacity in the face of that scathing sarcasm.

"This," said the unknown—and, taking off his glove, he showed Ulric a black and bloody hand. "It's from this hand, which you believed buried forever beneath the chapel, that Wilhelm, the avaricious peasant you punished so well, snatched the manuscript that he regarded as a sovereign talisman." In a mocking voice, he added; "Do you want further proofs?"

"Enough! Enough!" exclaimed Ulric, putting his hands over his eyes. "I know you now; you're . . ."

"A great lord who desires to maintain his incognito for the moment. Furthermore, loving the arts and poetry, occupying myself a little with architecture and chemistry, but without personal preoccupations, I leave all the glory and profit of my works to a few elite men that I have chosen from the crowd, and whose anonymous collaborator I deign to be in order not to wound their modesty."

"And what do you ask of those whom you heap with your gifts?" asked Ulric, going pale. "Doubtless some sacrilegious condition—some monstrous profanation, like the one you imposed on your victims who are asleep beneath the flagstones of Cologne cathedral! Back, accursed one! At that price I don't want the dishonest glory that you give and the poisoned fruits with which you heap your worshipers!"

The unknown's eyes blazed in a manner so terrible that the profound shadows of the room seemed momentarily dissipated. He soon resumed his cold and implacable irony, however.

"That's typical of the ingrate and cowardly race of Adam, coveting the tree of life with their eyes, but not daring to take it in their hand! Glory and fortune, those two fruits gilded by time, you want to pick in a day, but without danger, and you play indignation before me! Look into your soul! Each of your thoughts is a crime. Look at your hands! They are stained with the blood of another ambitious and avaricious poltroon, but one less guilty than you! And you don't want to be mine, you say—but you bent your knee before my power on the day when fraud and murder entered your heart! Bow that head, then, in which the seeds I deposited there have flourished so well . . . and you'll raise it proud and before the crowd that awaits you. But think! Your response will make you Ulric, the sovereign and respected poet before whom the hearts of women beat more rapidly, or Ulric the murderer, forger and thief, who conquered his titles to genius at the point of a dagger!"

During this speech, the young man's terror had increased to horror. The unknown's final words seemed to have given a substance to his crime, and each of his thoughts appeared to him as a spirit of darkness dragging him toward the gulf.

Footsteps were audible in the corridor; it was doubtless Franck coming to look for his friend.

"Bow down, adore me and go enjoy your renown and the sensualities that await you!" said the stranger, in a strident and curt voice.

"Never!" cried Ulric, launching himself toward the other side of the room, where he had just perceived an ivory Christ which seemed to be inviting him to shelter in its protective shadow. "Back, king of the abyss! It is written: Thou shalt worship no other than the Lord thy God!"

And, matching gesture to words, he threw himself to his knees before the sacred symbol.

The footsteps in the corridor were drawing nearer and nearer. The joyful voice of Max could be heard, who seemed to be already enjoying his friend's triumph.

The unknown uttered a terrible roar on seeing his victim prostrate before the Christ, the vanquisher of death and Hell. His handsome features, in which a few traces still showed on an eclipsed divine splendor, contracted in a manner so horrible that the young man uttered a cry of fright and fell unconscious at the foot of the cross at the exact moment when Franck opened the door noisily.

The cry of anguish uttered by Ulric had such a character of terror that Franck came into the room shivering, fearful of some mishap. The cry had chilled the very marrow in his bones. However, placing his candle on the mantelpiece, he ran to his friend, whom he found unconscious, his features imprinted with a mortal terror. Large droplets of cold sweat were bathing his hair and temples.

"Ulric! Ulric!" cried Franck, placing his friend's head against his bosom. "It's me, it's Franck, your brother!"

Ulric opened wild and staring eyes; his hand seemed to be pushing something odious away with an instinctive movement.

Finally, the cares of Max and Franck recalled him to reason and to life.

"Oh, don't abandon me! Don't leave me, I implore you!" cried the unfortunate young man, clinging to his friends.

Then, throwing himself on his knees before the sovereign cross that had broken the power of the unknown, he gave aloud before his frightened friends the confession of his crime and his culpable fraud.

"God has forgiven you, since he has protected you," said Franck. "Be calm and strong, then. Repentance is a celestial armor against which Satan can do nothing. But let's hasten to quit this house, where your cries have raised alarm. You, Max, go and give our friend's excuses to the assembly, saying that a terrible indisposition has overwhelmed him suddenly and will not permit him to realize his hopes today."

"Neither today, nor tomorrow, nor ever!" cried Ulric, hotly. "And to prove it to you, I'll deliver to the flames that accursed book in which the demon adopted the divine voice of genius in order to seduce me!"

Franck stopped Ulric's hand, which was already reaching toward the table to seize the mysterious book, and picked it up himself, pushed by a instinctive impulse of curiosity. He opened it. . . .

The pages were all blank, except for a large bloodstain on the first leaf.

"Ulric!" sad Franck, frightened. "God has preserved you for great things, since he has permitted you to be subjected to such a proof! Remember the specter of the nameless tomb! That one also wanted the glory without the toil, and collected nothing but oblivion and an eternal anathema. In this book, where you read triumphs yesterday, you will no longer find anything today but the bloody trace of your crime."

In 1840, a few months after that event, which had severely shaken Ulric's health, we saw the unfortunate young man in Cologne, his reason still unsteady under the terrible shock it had received. Franck and Max, those noble and loyal German hearts, finally brought peace and repose back to the poor soul that had seen at close range the gulf in which so many others have been lost without return.

Strangely enough, all the copies of the fragment of the dramatic trilogy of the Nibelungen that Ulric had had printed are, at the present moment, irredeemably lost. All the researches of antiquaries and bibliophiles have remained without result.

The traveler who passes today through the bleakest part of Franconia, and who goes into the monastery of Moratz will hear mention of a monk whose name is blessed every day by all those who weep and are suffering.

That monk, who bears on his face, paled by penitence and expiation, the traces of a terrible struggle, is Ulric.

THE END OF A STORY OF WHICH THE BEGINNING IS FAMILIAR

THERE are two things that have always occupied me greatly, since I have understood that one of the great joys of life is to sway in a soft hammock, while reading some naïve and charming storyteller, whose brilliant fantasy steals you away to the marvelous land of dreams. The first is knowing what became of the heroes of romances and fairy tales.

The second of my preoccupations is even more serious than the first, and above all, less futile; and any man who occupies himself in his hours of leisure with ameliorating the lot of his fellows will understand it marvelously. Thus, I would gladly renounce my political rights to the glory of being immortalized in a biography at two francs a line, and a host of other sensualities just as poignant in order to know what has become of: the ring of Solomon, which put Hell in commotion like the sound of the master's bell resounding in the antechamber; the hat of Fortunatus, by means of which one can arrive in China on the eve of one's departure; Astolfo's hippogriff; the horse Bayard and Roland's Durandal; Aladdin's lamp; and the marvelous ring

of Gyges, by means of which one could write such curious memoirs on the private lives of our great men and the
real beauties of some of our great ladies. Finally, I would
give all the oratory talent of Monsieur de Lamartine to
have news of Robin Hood's bow, Agramante's sword, the
horse of the four sons of Aymon, the boots worn by Perrault's Puss-in-Boots and the seven league boots of that
poor devil of an ogre who was so treacherously mystified
by that imp Petit Poucet, who professed such little voca-
tion to be eaten as a toothsome morsel.

Let someone show me, in the matters that are the object
of the investigations of contemporary science, subjects
more worthy of exercising the sagacity and intelligence
of academies and royal commissions, or even patent of-
fices! Show me endeavors more useful to the wellbeing of
humankind than those that might be rediscovered in the
lumber-room of a bric-à-brac merchant or in the ragged
and dusty chaos of a second-hand clothing store: one of
those charming magic wands by means of which the impossible is obtained without difficulty, and which rehabili-
tate the absurd by realizing instantaneously the craziest,
most curious and most grotesque caprices!

Now, people would listen to me with a religious attention, and silence would fall upon the political and literary
world, if I were to make my contemporaries party to an
unparalleled discovery that proves to what extent one can
add faith to the tales of Perrault, who has been classified,
until now, among those ingenious narrators for whom the
truth is only a matter of very secondary importance.

✳

There are people who choose, in order to see the sea, a day when the pure and profound sky offers not a wisp of cloud, when the winds, consigned to their cavern, cease to trouble the vast oceanic solitudes, where the calm and disarmed waves no longer bear the plumes of foam that undulate on their roaring summits on the days of conflict when the old Ocean seems to be scaling the sky. What is required by those tourists, people of order and peace, is a sea that reflects the eternal flat calm of their souls. A wrinkle in the waves, a patch of mist in the sky, and that is their pleasure spoiled, lost! As for us, we profess, in matters of maritime contemplation, entirely opposite theories; we do not like to see "old father Ocean," as the English say, in bourgeois Sunday clothing, well combed, neat and tidy, fearful of crumpling, by virtue of an abrupt movement, the white folds of his underwear.

We only like the sea in its colossal wrestling-matches with the north wind, when both are howling and bellowing like antediluvian leviathans. We love to see the roaring waves racing from the depths of the horizon like a pack of lions shaking their gray manes and launching themselves toward the summit over every rock, which they seem to want to take by storm. We like the sea when the hurricane labors it with its powerful wing and hollows out vast grooves therein, in the midst of which the sea-mews and petrels play. An angry sea is, for us, the most terrifying and the most imposing of God's marvels; a placid and flat sea is nothing but a wide road open to grocers, on which galleys laden with rice or coffee make ponderous progress, or broad-bellied barges stuffed with herrings and cheese.

So, a few months ago, the weather seemed to us to be entirely propitious to go and pay our tribute of admiration to the wrathful Ocean. In Brussels, it was raining chimney-pots and stove-pipes, which gave us to understand than in Ostend the wind must be blowing hard enough to rip the horns off a buffalo. The sea must have been beautiful and imposing, and the concert of the wind and waves promised magnetic effects that the modern makers of pianos have not yet found a means of imitating, even by breaking twenty pedals.

A week after that thought had crossed our mind, we were in the dunes near Blankenberghe, and if our admiration had been forced to take a voice, it would only have been able to join in with the wheeling chorus of marine birds saluting the tempest with cries of joy. The black and heavy sky was confounded at the limits of the horizon with the somber ones of the Ocean. An amber line, drowned in gray vapors, indicated the place where the sun was disappearing at every instant behind the clouds that followed one another rapidly and furiously, like black airborne battalions. Over the sea, the battle was even more furious and disordered. The north wind was twisting into foamy spirals the waves that were battering the shore, while in the distance, waves like frenzied mares could be seen hurtling toward the shore, growling and roaring with clamors to deafen a lover of Verdi's operas.

Sometimes, the bellowing of the hurricane redoubled in fury, and the noise of the waves drowned out the voice of the thunder. A somber mist extended between the sea and the sky, as if to veil the battle of the spirits of the abyss against the genii of the air. Furious wave-crests sharpened by the hurricane seemed at times to want to come and snatch me from the beach, and fell at my feet growling like muzzled and impotent monsters: all that noise, movement, clamor, fury and foam! It was grandiose and beautiful, enough to make one fall to one's knees and adore God in his supreme work of force and immensity.

"By God!" I cried. "This is weather that ought to depress the shares of insurance companies as much as the barometer. Old Father Aeolus has tipped out his bag in order to send to the charge his merest zephyrs, those that are still, like Papefiguiere's little devil, hailing on the parsley! At much moments, it's better, as Panurge said, to be a planter of cabbages on land that an emperor at sea![1] May God protect the cod. . . !"

"And those who bring it to us," said a voice behind me.

"That's what I was about to add, when you interrupted me, friend," I said, to a sort of mariner whose arrival the noise of the waves had prevented me from hearing. "When I shouted 'God protect the cod!'" I said, resuming my speech, "I meant the cod for which we're waiting and those who will bring it to us, because the cod that are yet to be caught can look after themselves."

"That's all right, Monsieur," said my companion, with a sigh, scrutinizing the horizon with his gaze. "Those who are at sea at present don't know where they'll wake up tomorrow."

"Have you some relative at sea? Are you waiting for a belated fishing-boat?"

"Alas, yes, Monsieur—that of my brother-in-law Jérôme, the handsomest fellow and the most adroit and intrepid fisherman on the coast. His wife is ill, and every gust of wind makes her shiver as if she saw him sinking,

---

1 Papefiguiere is, like Panurge, a character from Rabelais.

body and soul. The poor woman spent the whole night praying; this morning, she had me summoned and begged me to come to the shore to see whether any fisherman's sail might be visible at sea. I told her that there was a wind to unbutton gaiters blowing at the coast, and that my presence wouldn't make her husband's boat arrive an hour sooner, but she didn't want to hear it, and here I am, Monsieur, waiting until God wants to bring my poor Jérôme back safe and sound. And you, Monsieur, you're doubtless waiting for someone?"

"Me! I've arrived from Brussels."

"Oh, I see—urgent business. For it must be, to stand on the shore in weather like this."

"My God no, my friend. When I see on the barometer that the sea is going to get somewhat annoyed, I put a dozen cigars in my pocket and I come to Blankenberghe. Would you care for a cigar, comrade?"

"With pleasure, Monsieur. And you've come from Brussels like that to see the rain, and to risk being carried away by the wind? That's a funny idea, because, you see, at this hour, there's hardly anyone outside but customs men and seagulls."

At that moment I saw a black dot appear in a gap in the sky, which disappeared a moment later, as if it had fallen into the curve of the wave that was carrying it.

"Look!" I cried, pointing at the point in the sky where I had just seen the black dot surge forth. "There's a boat coming back, and I don't see why it shouldn't be your brother-in-law's!"

"May Our Lady of Hanswyck hear you, Monsieur!" said my companion.

And, taking off his cap, he knelt down, and I saw his lips muttering a fervent prayer.

I know nothing more frankly pious than a sailor. Always confronting death, his confidence in God is far more profound and energetic than that of men parked in cities, where one only perceives the works of God between the summits of houses. A patch of sky, gray or dappled with soot: that, for the bourgeois, is the specimen of the marvels of Providence, so it isn't astonishing that he's a Voltairean and a strong mind, until his first attack of gout or apoplexy.

Soon, we saw distinctly, surging between the foamy crests of the waves, the tip of a mast, where a flame floated, which seemed, a moment later, to be swallowed by the void formed by the waves. My companion's eyes followed those oscillations anxiously, which made us pass from terror to hope. Finally, the entire mast was slowly disengaged from the furious grip of the waves, and we soon saw the brown sails of a fishing boat that was flying toward the shore with a frightful velocity.

"God be praised!" said my companion. "It's my brother-in-law Jérôme; I recognize his patched sails and his striped tiller. If you'd like, Monsieur, to stay here until he's landed, you'd give me great pleasure; tell him that his brother-in-law Jean came to make sure of his arrival, and that he's gone to inform his sister of her husband's return."

I promised the honest fisherman to comply with his instructions, and he drew away, running toward the village and leaving me alone on the strand.

The boat was running with the wind behind it with a rapidity that made me anxious for its safety, all the more so as the surf of the waves unfurling on the coast was terrible. Suddenly, the wind veered to the east; the boat took advantage of that moment to haul in its sails, and a prudent and expert maneuver soon brought it close to shore, where an enormous wave deposited it gently on the strand.

Two men dressed in tarred canvas jackets and coiffed in leather caps leapt nimbly to the ground and moored the boat firmly to pylons profoundly fixed in the sand. Both were streaming with sea-water and simulating quite well, save for the salt water, pagan river-gods ready to attend some masked ball.

"Halloo the boat!" I shouted. "Is the master named Jérôme, and are you coming back from cod fishing?"

"I'm Jérôme—what do you want with me?" said one of the men.

"Then set a course this way, comrade; I have something to tell you"

"Give me time to moor this cable, and I'm yours, Monsieur. I don't want a wave to pick up my boat and take it to Newfoundland, from which it's just arrived, by the grace of God!"

Two minutes later, the master of the boat was beside me on the dune. He was a handsome and vigorous fellow between thirty and thirty-five years old, with an athletic stature, square shoulders, sturdy and muscular legs, and a limpid gaze, bold and soft at the same time. His face, animated by toil and lashed by the hurricane, radiated a contained interior joy.

The man had been tanned and bronzed by all the winds of the compass and tempered by the thunder of twenty tempests. He had the masculine authority of the mariner whose childhood has been rocked by the hurricane and whose maturity has been an everyday struggle with the formidable Ocean, the furies of which human science is impotent to muzzle and its wrath impossible to tame.

"As you don't know me, my brave fellow," I said to the fisherman, "I'll tell you briefly that your brother-in-law quit the shore a moment ago, to go and inform your wife, who was mortally anxious, of your safe arrival."

"And you stayed on the coast in weather like this to give me that good news, Monsieur?"

"But it seems to me, comrade, that the one of us exposed to more risk wasn't me. I had a solid beach beneath my feet, while I was trembling at every moment to see those furious waves engulf your nutshell."

"You call that a nutshell!" said the fisherman, pointing with pride at his moored boat, whose keel was being licked by the waves. "It's obvious that you bourgeois, habituated to perch in plaster cages, don't understand our métier." He enveloped his vessel with an amorous gaze. "But with that nutshell, I can make a tour of the world as quickly as Captain Petit's *Louise*."[1]

Evidently, without intending to, I had wounded the fisherman's pride, and, doubtless unwittingly, he had profoundly humiliated me by calling me bourgeois. We were, therefore, quits, so I resumed the conversation without any kind of rancor.

"When I said nutshell, my brave Jérôme, I didn't mean any offense to your boat; I was merely afraid, on seeing her at odds with such a monstrous sea, of seeing her break like one of those pleasure-yachts made for navigating in a goldfish bowl."

1 The French naval officer Abel Aubert du Petit Thouars (1793-1864) captured *La Louise-Marie*, known familiarly as the *Petite Louise*, in 1833 during a conflict against the Peruvians; he or a relative—he belonged to a considerable naval family—subsequently employed the vessel in transporting Belgian colonists to Guatemala, hence its role in Belgian legendry.

"Have you ever heard of a cod or a sturgeon drowning in a tempest?" said my fisherman, with a mocking expression.

"I've read a great many newspapers, but I confess that I've never encountered a disaster of that kind."

"Well, I've seen whales cast up by a heavy sea on Dogger Bank, and leaving their skin and lard there, while the little fish lifted up by a wave return with it to the open sea, from which they hasten to return to their lodgings. And that's what proves to you that if my nutshell had been a ship with three decks, tacking a league from the coast, with the wind behind and all sails hoisted, she'd be covering the strand with her debris at this moment, and I wouldn't be eating supper this evening with my wife, and wouldn't have the pleasure of accompanying you to Blankenberghe."

"And you haven't suffered any other damage than a few tattered sails?" I said, pointing at a jib in which the wind had made several long rips.

"A little broken rigging, a few torn sails, that's all the tempest could do to me . . . oh, I was forgetting an old pair of fishing-boots that a splash of sea-water carried away. I ask you, what can it do with an old pair of fishing-boots? But let's make haste, or the night will surprise us; we'll chat on the way."

"In fact," I said, matching strides with the fisherman, "it's funny, after all. Who knows? At this moment, your boots might be inhabited by an honest family of herrings that have sought a refuge there from the rapacity of sharks."

"Oh, you think that a shark respects boots?" said my fisherman, bursting into laughter. "I'll tell you what happened to me with one of those starvelings, for which anything is good. I was aboard a whaler off the coast of Chile. A sly shark was following us like a poodle, trying all sorts of tricks to get hold of a morsel of no matter what, for those parishioners eat anything at all. We baited a hook with an old pretty officer's cap; we threw the cable in the water; a minute later, the cap, the hook and two feet of chain had disappeared into the throat of our amiable guest. We let him get a good grip and then we hoisted him aboard, where everyone got in a blow, one with a knife, another with a pike, a third with a hatchet. A sailor opened the belly and the stomach, and guess what we found. . . ."

"An entire English family: three damsels in green veils, four boys, two chambermaids, a coachman and a groom in yellow gaiters, no doubt," I said, with a serious expression.

"If you think I'm joking, let's say no more," said Jérôme, in a semi-annoyed fashion.

"My God!" I said. "If you think, because you're a mariner and I'm a bourgeois, as you put it, that you're going to make me believe stories. . . ."

"What I'm going to tell you is as true as my name's Jérôme. So, a sailor opened the shark's stomach, and as the weather was set fair and the captain was in a good mood, the sailor proposed to make a regular inventory of the shark's stomach; another suggested that we seize the shark's furniture. We settled on that idea as the more amusing. So, my man installed himself in the glutton's stomach, and I got a pen in order to draw up the legal document, which began like that of a bailiff; after that came the *items*, and there were a lot of them: item, two twenty-four bullets and a fur bonnet; item, one parrot-cage; item, one night-bag containing toilet necessities; item, one straw hat;

item, one tin can, well-sealed, full of smoked beef; item, three pairs of trousers and two navy jackets; a Bible and a compass; two shoes and one boot, and a collection of gazettes, and other affairs that proved that the shark had traveled a great deal and had been content with everything that Providence had sent him."

At that moment we reached the first houses of Blankenberghe; my companion quit me, giving me a cordial handshake and saying: "If the fancy takes you some day to make an excursion at sea, ask for me. Try, above all, to make sure that there's a good breeze, not a flat and torpid sea such as the bourgeois desire who come here to count their shirts and catch colds in the head."

I promised Jérôme to come and remind him of the promise he'd just made very soon, and two hours later, I found myself in Bruges, admiring the magnificent belfry, a formidable symbol of the eclipsed power of our glorious Flemish communes.

While my thoughts were caressing amorously the marvelous architectonics in which the palace is allied with the citadel, and the damp black prison rubs shoulders with the vast hall with sculpted paneling gilded like a picture-frame, my gaze fell upon a second-hand clothes shop, on the hooks of which hung all kinds of faded garments, holed and soiled specters in which a few traces could still be discovered of a former luxury. Formerly varnished riding-boots were colliding with hob-nailed shoes. Pink satin hats were mourning their past splendor alongside a civil guard shako. It was a necropolis of phantoms of clothing and footwear, which seemed to be saying to me: *Hodie mihi, cras tibi.*[1]

----

1 Today it's me; tomorrow it'll be you.

To fall from the gracious trefoils that form a crown of gold and azure on the forehead of the majestic belfry to the philosophical contemplation of the shop was a steep decline, but I know not what stupid and idle disposition brought me to examine in detail all the tattered antiquities that were displaying their misery beneath a stray sunbeam shining through a gap in the clouds.

Suddenly, my gaze fell on an old pair of boots in a very poor state, but whose ancient and obsolete form must have condemned them to float for years in the dealer's display. Those boots bore no resemblance to contemporary boots; they were neither hunting-boots, nor military boots, nor riding-boots. The foot was wider than usual, the stem hard and strong; in sum, they resembled the boots that Sterne gave to Uncle Toby, although I would not dare to affirm too much. At the top of the stem was a funnel such a Vandermeulen gave to his cavaliers.[1]

The merchant, who saw me in contemplation before those boots, which had seen at least two generations pass, doubtless mistook me for an Englishman idling away the time while awaiting his dinner hour, or some collector occupied in accumulating footwear of every kind, from the sandal, the caliga and the espadrille to the gaitered brodequin invented by our ingenious epoch. For myself, I was thinking about poor Jérôme, whose fishing-boots had been carried away by a surge of the sea, and meditating some great munificence that would cause my name to be blessed on the coast of Blankenberghe unto the third generation.

---

1 "Uncle Toby" is Toby Shandy, the uncle of the hero of Laurence Sterne's *Tristram Shandy* (1759-67). The second reference is to the Baroque painter Adam Frans van der Meulen (1632-1690), who became Louis XIV's official battle painter.

There we were, the clothes-dealer and I, observing one another, me seeking the means to make the best possible bargain for the ridiculous boots that I was not at all sure how I would carry away if he let me have them at a reasonable price, and him trying to read in my eyes what mysterious interest could be moving me to make that purchase.

Finally, I decided to break the silence.

"Those are singular boots, friend," I said, with an expression full of superb scorn, touching the horrible tubes of the boots with the tip of my cane.

"Yes, Monsieur," said the clothes-dealer, in an insouciant tone. "They weren't made yesterday, those; I found them in my father's shop."

"And you'll probably transmit them with your succession to your son."

"If I don't sell them beforehand, it's quite possible, for it won't be me who'll wear them out."

"I can believe that! Who the Devil do you expect to wear boots of that sort? They're only good to hang in a cabinet of antiquities. How much do you want for them?"

"Ten francs," said the merchant in a dry tone, plunging his eyes into mine, to see the effect that the exorbitant demand would have on me.

There's a proudly circumcised Christian, I thought, privately. *He definitely takes me for an Englishman.*

An offer of six francs touched the clothes-dealer's heart, and, furnished with my boots, which attracted the gazes of all the passers-by, I returned to my hotel.

The next day, when I woke up, my first thought was to inform myself as to the condition of the sky. Somber clouds fringed with an amber border were racing across a heavy and misty sky. The wind was fresh and on the coast the conditions ought to be found that had been demanded by Jérôme for an excursion at sea. The waves ought to be restive beneath their mane of foam, and the wind sighing through the rigging.

Let's go show that exterminator of sharks and conqueror of cod, who seemed to be mocking me yesterday, I thought, *that a bourgeois, as he dared to call me, doesn't recoil before a nice stiff breeze.*

When I arrived at Jérôme's house, I was told that he was on the beach supervising the unloading of his boat, and would be returning before long. In fact, half an hour had not gone by when I saw him arrive, carrying a torn sail over his shoulder, which he was going to replace with a spare jib. On seeing me he started with surprise.

"I've come to summon you to keep the promise you made me yesterday. The wind's fresh; we can idle for an hour or two at sea. But in order that you don't lose the fruit of your time, which is your capital, as it's also mine, I've brought you a pair of boots to replace those that the sea fished off your boat. What do you think of my idea?"

"I say that you're a brave fellow," said the honest mariner, shaking my hand as if to break it. "I say that to prove how grateful I am for this gift, I'll take you out to sea, when all the winds of the north-west are unleashed, and I'll bring you back to land without your getting a thread wet!"

While the loyal fisherman was expressing his energetic gratitude thus, I unpacked the boots, not without some anxiety as to the reception my acquisition might obtain. But without taking the trouble to examine them, he picked one up, took off his shoe and put on the boot, which seemed to me to have been made for him. He pulled up the funnel, which came up to his groin. The leather, which had seemed as hard and refractory as iron the day before, was now as supple as deerskin, and lent itself to all the forms and movements of the legs and feet.

Well, I thought, *my thief of a clothes-merchant has a conscience—he's greased his antiques with fish-oil. That's a wise precaution against sea-water.*

"So," I said to Jérôme, who seemed ecstatic with his boots, "you're content with my acquisition?"

"So much so that they couldn't have shod me more comfortably if you'd had them made for my foot! And what leather! How soft, supple and solid it is!"

"I'm delighted that you're satisfied with them—but let's not waste time. I'll wait for you on the shore; go get what you need and wear your boots for the first time in my honor."

"As you say!" exclaimed Jérôme, joyfully. "I'll go show your gift to my wife, get a sheet for my jib, and I'll be with you in five minutes."

I walked to the strand with the feeling of wellbeing that a good deed gives. One thing, however, preoccupied my mind and intrigued me singularly: those boots, which I had seen the day before rigid, hard and inflexible, as dry and wrinkled as the skin of an old maid who has accumulated forty springs while waiting for a husband; those boots that I had feared seeing refused even by a simple fisherman, so grotesque and inhospitable were they, I had seen become supple, embellished, taking on a freshness they had not possessed the day before. There was something in that that my mind could not explain, unless by supposing that the clothes-dealer, ashamed of having robbed me unworthily, had made it a case of conscience to restore them carefully to newness.

The sight of the Ocean soon changed the course of my thoughts. The sea, stirred by a brisk southerly breeze, was shiny under the saffron-tinted rays of a pale sun. Seagulls searching for some meager fry were gliding over the crests of the waves, skimming them with their brown wings. The beach was bordered by a fringe of foam and the waves were dying there with a melancholy sound conducive to drowsiness and reverie. Sometimes, a cloud, chased by the wind, passed in front of the sun and abruptly extinguished all those maritime splendors in which each wave bore a feathery tuft sparkling with carbuncles or rubies on its head. A moment later, a gap in the clouds covered the surface of the Ocean once again with a dazzling carpet of gold over which the waves detached their white fleeces of foam. It was charming and sublime, imposing and graceful, enough to make one desert forever the abode of a city to come and live in some hole in the dunes.

The five minutes requested by my friend Jérôme were beginning to seem long, however. Perhaps an hour had gone by during my contemplative ecstasy. I attributed my companion's delay to one of those important stupidities that always hinder the most serious matters at the last moment: a thread for which one searches, a pipe that one breaks, a lighter that one forgets. Any of those trivial things could have delayed my brave shark-killer.

I sat down on the beach, and lit a second cigar, promising myself to quit the spot as soon as it was consumed. Waiting for a man for the duration of two cigars is a politeness from which a Chinaman would recoil, even if he were a red-button mandarin.

I waited for a second hour, during which my thoughts, absorbed by the immensity and the grandeur of the spectacle that unfurled before me, seemed to have quit my body. Rapid choirs of marine birds were circling in the joyous sunlight, uttering shrill cries. The somnolent harmony of the waves that came to caress the strand was beginning to act upon me. I got up abruptly and returned to Blankenberghe, to discover what was delaying Jérôme.

When I arrived at his house, his wife manifested a profound surprise at his absence. She thought he was at sea with me.

"He left two hours ago, Monsieur," she told me, with a secret anxiety. "He came to show me the beautiful boots that you were generous enough to give him. He took his pipe and told me that he was going to buy a sheet for his jib, and then join you immediately on the beach."

"But I've just come from the beach, my good woman. I've been waiting there for two hours."

"If my husband were vainglorious," the fisherman's wife said to me, smiling, "I could believe that he was in some tavern, busy having his boots admired, but he said to me as he went out: 'Wife, I'm going to get a bit of cable from the grocer, and then I'll go find the monsieur I promised to take for an excursion at sea. I'll be back for supper at four o'clock.'"

"Bah!" I said, heading for the door. "That will have to be postponed. Your husband must have had some urgent and unexpected business that has prevented him from keeping his promise. I'll come back tomorrow; tell him that I don't hold any rancor against him for his delay."

As I left the fisherman's wife I met some of his colleagues, whom I asked for news of Jérôme. No one had seen him; his brother-in-law searched all the taverns and gin-houses in the vicinity without being able to discover any trace of him. I went to the shore; he had not appeared and his boat, still moored, was bobbing on the waves awaiting us.

That disappearance, without being worrying, was nevertheless singular, all the more so as Jérôme was known to be an orderly, sober man with a down-to-earth humor, not given to going astray. Nevertheless, as the most mysterious and bizarre events almost always end up finding a simple and natural explanation, I soon ceased to think about my fisherman and returned to Bruges.

The following day, as I was about to quit the melancholy Venice of the North, nowadays as sad and desolate as its sister in the Adriatic, the abrupt and singular disappearance of the fisherman came back to my mind. It seemed to me that I owed those worthy folk a visit, if only to assure myself that nothing unfortunate had happened to the honest Jérôme, who had manifested such a keen gratitude for a small gift, and had offered, in order to oblige me, to confront the gracious westerly winds that we had heard roaring in our chimneys and howling outside our shaking windows in recent days.

I therefore decided to make one final visit to my brave cod-fisherman. I don't know what secret instinct told me that the meeting might tell me strange, bizarre things and that I would not have to repent of the few hours sacrificed to a visit that, after all, had its source in a solicitude of which the honest Jérôme was well worthy.

When I arrived in Blankenberghe I noticed among the neighbors and comrades of my fisherman the anxious and feverish activity that always follows events somewhat outside the ordinary course of things. Women were gathered in groups, chattering on doorsteps; men were talking to one another with gestures full of the telegraphic mobility that one finds among Neapolitans and the people of the Midi. Sometimes, profound shrugs of the shoulders seemed to summarize the conversations, as if the orators were admitting that they did not understand anything of the subject of discussion that was preoccupying them.

At the sight of me, the whisperings redoubled, and twenty tarry index fingers were directed toward me with mysterious murmurs. The groups tightened and drew away as I approached, as if I were a leper, a plague-carrier or a bearer of arrest warrants. Slightly discomfited by those demonstrations and that welcome, I nevertheless marched with a firm tread to Jérôme's house; I opened the door and the first thing that struck my gaze was the fisherman, lying in bed and prey to an ardent fever.

My sudden appearance produced a prodigious effect. A few neighbors and the invalid's wife, who were surrounding the bed, recoiled in terror toward the wall, as if they wanted to sink into it.

"Why the Devil are you all looking at me like that with such fearful expressions?" I said to the assembly. "Have I perhaps forgotten to take off my night-cap when I got up this morning?"

A profound silence greeted my words. All gazes looked in turn at me and the fisherman, whose sleep appeared to be troubled by some feverish dream.

Suddenly, the invalid woke up abruptly, and, seeing me beside him, uttered a cry of astonishment and amazement.

"Ah! There you are, finally," he said, in a voice that he sought to render menacing. "You can boast of having caused me to voyage in an unexpected, economical manner, and without a spare pair of socks!"

Decidedly, I thought, *the poor devil has lost his head; his imagination is wandering without sail or compass over the vast sea of the absurd.*

"Alas, Monsieur," the fisherman's wife said to me, "I don't know what's wrong with my husband, but since he came back to the house this morning he's been making the most extravagant speeches, talking about things that, saving your respect, don't make any sense."

"It's you who don't know what you're saying," said Jérôme, in an irritated tone. "Get out, all of you! I need to talk to Monsieur for an hour, so that he can explain to me . . ."

"I'll explain anything you wish, my good Jérôme," I said to the fisherman, trying to calm him down, "but first promise me to be tranquil and not to cause your friends alarm by being as irritated and ill-tempered as you seem."

"I'll do whatever they like," said the invalid, "but before anything else, let them leave us alone. I have to say things to you, Monsieur, that you alone ought to hear."

I made a sign with my hand to those present to go, in order to leave me alone with the fisherman, and when the door was closed, this is the strange story that he told me.

A VOYAGE OF CIRCUMPEREGRINATION AROUND THE WORLD AND EVEN FURTHER
by Jérôme Axël
Cod-Fisherman of Blankenberghe

"Before beginning the tale of my travels," said Jérôme, "I need, Monsieur, to give you all the possible guarantees that I really am in full possession of my reason. That's indispensable to the story I'm going to tell you. In consequence, do me the pleasure of imposing on me any proof you please. Would you like me to recite my *Pater*, carry out an operation in arithmetic, tell you how many leagues there are between Blankenberghe and the Faroë Islands, or the banks of Newfoundland? Do as you like, in order that you won't suppose, when I've finished, that you've been listening seriously to the nonsense of a brain whipped by fever."

In the fisherman's speech there was a calm so intelligent, a reason so cold and so self-confident, that I promised to add to his words the belief that I would give to a relation of a voyage authorized by the government and certified veritable by the ship's log and the sworn testimony of the crew.

After having collected himself for a few minutes, Jérôme commenced thus:

"You know, Monsieur, that you quit me at the moment when I was going into my house to invite my wife to admire the famous boots that you had had the generosity of bringing me from Bruges. After having shown your gift to my wife, who could not get over that generosity of a stranger to whom I had only talked once, I took my boots under my arm, lit my pipe and told my wife that I would be back about four o'clock, or five at the latest.

"Having arrived in the street, I told myself that it was ridiculous to carry one's boots under one's arm, especially when they were as finely turned as mine; so I sat down on the bench outside my door, and put them on, in order to go to the grocery of sorts where I ought to find a new sheet for my jib. I took a step . . .

"Imagine my surprise, my astonishment and my terror! I found myself in the middle of a field, far from any house, no longer able to see the bell-tower of Blankenberghe or that of Notre Dame de Bruges, which is five hundred feet high. I stopped, believing that I was prey to the illusion of some mirage, or, to tell you the truth, that I was seeing things. I rubbed my eyes, I looked . . . the country surrounding me was perfectly unknown to me!

"At that sight, my head was troubled. I launched myself forward, I ran—and, astonishingly, at every step, the landscape, the aspect of the country and the forms of habitations changed their appearance. I saw the earth fleeing under my feet like the surface of a rapidly-spinning mill-wheel. The streams, the roads, the houses and the trees went past me with the velocity and the vague forms that objects have in dreams. It seemed to me at times that I was a living arrow launched by some monstrous arbalest, or a bipedal tug traveling at 12,600 leagues an hour.

"The most astonishing thing is that that incredible speed, compared to which the finest steamboat is only a Dutch barge, didn't hinder my respiration at all. On the contrary, I experienced an unknown wellbeing, a pleasure I'd never felt before.

"Finally, I stopped, and to assure myself that I wasn't dreaming, I bit the palm of my right hand here—look, the tooth-marks are still there! The pain I felt made me understand that I really was awake, and yet, around me, everything had changed again.

"I addressed myself to a man that I saw herding a flock of sheep in front of him, and asked the way to Blankenberghe. 'We have Bamberg, Heidelberg, Freiberg and Mulhberg,' the man replied, in a German language that made my hair stand on end.

"The country where I found myself had nothing that reminded me of Belgium. At my feet ran a broad river dominated by mountains, on the summits of which one could see ruined castles. God of mercy! I was in Germany, but where? In what country? Prussia, Swabia, Bavaria or Hungary? At that thought, my head was troubled, and I ran straight ahead, as if to escape the vertigo that was taking possession of my poor brain. But the more I ran, the more it seemed to me that I was going astray, and the more the mountains, the rivers, the cities and the villages fled before me as if in a flash of lightning. This time, though, it wasn't just the country that took on another character; everything, including the costume of the inhabitants, had changed completely!

"The country into the midst of which I found myself transported, or in which I seemed to be dreaming that I found myself, was punctuated by mountains, some of which were covered in snow at the summit. However, in the plain where I was running like a madman, the heat was overwhelming. The men that I was passing were wearing loose robes and turbans, and smoking long pipes.

"I was beginning to understand that there was something diabolical at the bottom of my affair. I made three signs of the cross, said my *Pater* and everything I could remember of my catechism, and I set forth.

"After a few minutes of walking that made me travel at the speed of a 36 bullet fired by a hunting rifle, I found myself on the edge of a strait where I saw a monsieur in a red hat with red hair, who was fishing with a line. 'Monsieur,' I said to him, 'in the name of your salvation, if you're a Christian, tell me the name of the country we're in and the name of the river in which you're fishing.'

"The man to whom I addressed that question raised his head slowly, looked at me for a few minutes as if to assure himself that I wasn't mad, and replied in good English: 'The country you're in is called Rumelia; the strait where

I'm fishing is called the Bosphorus, a Greek word that signifies *Ox-Ford*—but perhaps you don't know Greek?'

"All of that was said to me with the insolent and mocking attitude that the English have toward foreigners. I thought that the animal of an Englishmen was making fun of me, all the more so as, knowing my geography well and having traveled a great deal, I had never heard mention of a country called Rumelia and a strait called the Ox-Ford.

"I was so irritated and exasperated by my adventure, that it wouldn't have taken much for me to send the insolent fellow to see how many fathoms of water there were in his Ox-Ford.

"It might have been midday. I had left Blankenberghe at half past ten. I thought about you, who were waiting for me on the coast for our excursion at sea; my adventure was beginning to surpass the bounds of a simple joke. I let myself fall on to a charming lawn a few paces from the Englishman, who was still fishing without catching anything, and I looked around.

"To my right, under a pure and profound sky, was a city that seemed to me to be four times as large as Bruges. An innumerable quantity of white bell-towers rose up in the middle of the city. To my left, a vast sea extended its somber and tumultuous waves. In front of me, on the other side of the straight, was a verdant shore planted with trees.

"*Let's see*, I thought. *I can't hide from myself that what's happening to me is one of those things that mark an epoch in a man's life; I'll interrogate that tawny-haired Englishman again, and if he replies to me as the others did, if it's true that, having left Blankenberghe at half past ten, I'm five hundred leagues from my bell-tower, my wife and my boat, then I'll make my decision and make a tour of the world before returning for dinner. I've got good boots and three francs in my pocket; that's more than I need.*

"'Sir,' I said to the Englishman, with the most honest expression I could put on, 'be good enough to tell me the name of the city that we can see beside us to the right.'

"'That city is called Stamboul in Turkish, but perhaps you don't know Turkish?'

"'Very little, sir, very little. I'm a cod-fisherman; I scarcely know more than the Faroë Islands, Shetland, Iceland, and the coasts of Norway, and in all those countries people don't make much use of Turkish. But to get back to my affair, the name of that sea one can see in the distance, whose waves seem so somber?'

"'That sea is the Pontos Euxios, which means *hospitable sea.*'

"I opened my eyes wide to look for that Pont Euxin, which should, at any rate, have been a goodly length,[1] but I couldn't see anything except waves and a few sails.

"*My Englishman is definitely making fun of me*, I thought. *Let's go enquire elsewhere.*

"I went along the coast to the left, still with the rapidity that made objects pass before me like a lightning flash in a dark cloud. I went around the sea to the north and traversed a chain of mountains where men in pointed bonnets were fighting soldiers in green uniforms with swords. After half an hour, during which I went around lakes, crossed rivers and mountains, I arrived in a great desert of sand, all covered in salt, where camels were running. Finally, I found a fertile plain, traversed by a river that bore boats with roofs fitted with bell-towers and a

---

1 Pont Euxin was the ancient Greek name of the Black Sea, but Jérôme mistakes the first word for the French *pont*, meaning bridge.

heap of monkey-tricks. I stopped to ask an indigene the name of the country where I was and that of the beautiful river that was ferrying all those diabolical palanquins, where one could see ugly fellows smoking on the poop deck, like those one finds in tea-shops in Bruges.

"The individual replied to me in English that the country was called Ta-Thsing-Koué[1] and the river the Houang-Ho. 'Thank you, friend,' I said. 'Now I'm further forward than before.'

"I headed southwards, crossed a river they called the Yang-Tseu-Kiang, and then another called the Irrawaddy. I crossed mountains and arrived, at about two o'clock, in an admirable country, a true paradise. I stopped at the door of a big building ornamented by all sorts of sculpted devilries. In the front there was an immense terrace covered with a carpet, on which a few individuals were sitting like Père Tropique,[2] who were looking at lovely girls, yellow as amber, and wearing gold rings that traversed their nostrils. The girls were occupied in dancing a sort of polka, which would have made the gamekeeper of Blankenberghe blush.

"God forgive me, Monsieur, but I've never seen anything as beautiful as the dancing of those girls! They twisted like boas and bounded like panthers, and all with looks and thrusts to put the devil in the body of a wooden saint.

---

1 This is the name credited to the Chinese Empire in a French translation of Heinrich von Klaproth's commentary on Chinese geography and cosmography published in 1833, reproduced in various other French texts of the period.
2 "Père Tropique" is the French name of the symbolic figure featured in maritime ceremonies of the kind known in English as "crossing the line" (i.e., the equator).

"The old men, who seemed to me to be the rich and well-to-do of the place, were watching the lovely girls from the corners of their eyes like cats stalking a bird. Suddenly, one of them raises his head, says a few words in the local language to a domestic the color of *café-au-lait*, and I recognize . . . you'll never guess!"

"How the devil to you expect me to guess, my good Jérôme?" I said, utterly bewildered by this singular odyssey.

"I recognized in one of the Brahmins, as they call their curés, a Jew, a water-merchant from Cologne and thereabouts, who owed me three francs from the last fair in Bruges,

"'Hey, brigand!' I cried, launching myself toward him—but I finished my phrase in the middle of a wood, where my sudden arrival frightened a troop of tigers that were asleep in the shade of the jungle.

"*Well then*, I said to myself, *since I definitely can't go where I want to, let's continue our route.*

"I turned to the north, then, veering westwards, I traversed charming countries, intercut with vast solitudes in which one could see the ruins of great cities. At about half past two, I arrived on a little tongue of land where engineers were occupied in surveying the terrain. They were still Englishmen!

"One of the workers, to whom I addressed myself for information told me that I was at that moment astride Asia and Africa, and that I had before me the Sahara desert, twelve hundred leagues of sand, where ostriches only lay boiled eggs. Below me was Ethiopia, Nubia and a heap of Moorish kingdoms. So I turned back and this time headed north. I stopped in Jerusalem to dine there standing up, for in the singular malady that had taken possession of me, I wouldn't have been able to go to pick up a bottle of wine or a piece of bread without finding myself transported I don't know how many leagues.

"After having had a bite to eat, I headed north. I know all the coasts that way from Cape North and Cape Nassau all the way to the Kara Sea, and I counted on following the Gulf of Bothnia and the coast of the Baltic, in order to be able to get home in time for dinner, so as not to worry my wife. It was a famous idea I had there, Monsieur, and yet that was what was to bring me ill-fortune by rendering me witness to things that I'll never forget!

"So, there I am, traveling along Syria and the Black Sea, admiring all the marvels that the good God has sown in those countries, which are inhabited by those rogues the Turks and Cossacks, who do no honor to their government if it puts them in uniform. The majority have no trousers and have never heard of an overcoat. I cross a heap of rivers, the Don, the Volga, what do I know? Black, misty, stupid rivers—not a flower or a bird on their desolate banks. Cossacks and birches, that's all the ornament of those regions.

"Finally, having arrived at the source of a river that discharges into the White Sea, I had to veer westwards in order to reach the Porsanger Gulf on the Baltic. An unfortunate idea came to me to push on to the pole to see for myself the famous Cap Siévero-Vostotschenoï, or Sacred Promontory,[1] at the end of which, I'd heard tell, one

____

1 Severovostochny, nowadays an administrative district in Russia, was originally the Russian name of a cape subsequently renamed Cape Chelyuskin in 1842 after the first man to reach it a hundred years earlier; it is the northernmost point of the Eurasian continent, still a quasi-fabulous location in 1857.

can see the axis of the world naked, like a spit traversing a pullet.

"As I got closer to the pole, the light of the sun became duller and more livid, and its oblique rays no longer conserved the power that vivifies everything. Around me, everything was arid and devastated by torrents and volcanoes. Brown rocks covered with thick, dark moss; streams profoundly encased, which rolled their icy waters between two bare banks where the earth showed its old bones nakedly; a black and heavy sky in which you could wash your hands, the clouds were so low and thick; a few meager reindeer pursued by bears that hadn't been fat for two months and whose ribs you could count; cranes and storks perched on one paw on the edge of a stream, waiting for their dinner to pass by; foxes of all colors that have never eaten a chicken—that's the picture of those charming polar regions that men dare to inhabit and even have the effrontery to call a fatherland!

"While I stopped to see a little of the detail of the joys of that amiable land, the sky darkened; torrents of snow, rain and melting ice soon fell, so thick and compact that I only just had time to hide under the projection of a rock at the foot of which I found myself. The thunder died away and started again twenty times a minute, as if the sky and the earth were crossing their lightning-bolts in a mighty duel.

"Bright flashes of lightning lit up the profound darkness that surrounded me. One of those flashes, which had nothing in common with the wan glimmers of our land, and even the tropics, enabled me to see, lying next to me, two white bears, trembling in all their paws, which didn't seem to have the slightest desire to eat me, so consternated were they.

"The heavy and humid air, and the fissures and caverns of the rocks, reverberated the rolls of thunder with a din that I'll never hear again, even if the whole of Mount Hecla collapses into the Icelandic Sea. It was too black to think of resuming my journey, and it was blowing so hard that a white bear wouldn't have ventured out. I therefore resigned myself to waiting in my hole for sunrise or one of those beautiful aurora boreales that replace it in the polar lands.

"An hour went by, during which the rocks, struck by lightning, were exploding all around; the icy rain and snow were still falling. My bears didn't budge, and seemed to be imploring my protection. Finally, a dawn, pale at first, which passed rapidly from orange to vivid crimson, came to chase away the darkness. My bears got up gravely and went back to their domicile without even looking at me. Soon, the sky was ablaze, and a sheaf of red and yellow rays was sparkling, bursting forth everywhere like bouquets of fireworks. Believe me, it was a beautiful spectacle, which made me bless and adore God for having rendered me witness to those imposing marvels.

"I got my bearings from the pole star, which was shining brightly, and after a few steps found myself on a very particular terrain where, by another enchantment no less inexplicable than the first, I saw with terror that I had completely lost the rapidity of locomotion that had enabled me to witness in a few hours so many various spectacles, and on which I had counted to get back for dinner before five o'clock, in order not to worry my wife.

"Around me everything was dark and arid, and had an aspect that chilled me with fear. The ground I was treading was formed by an iron bar that appeared to me to be at least a league in diameter, and whose extremity reposed in a formidable rock whose base was lost in the darkness. From the place where I was I could see the earth turning with a prodigious rapidity, and I heard the colossal axle screeching on its granite support with hoarse noises that chilled the marrow in my bones.

"Above me and below me, everything was dark and dead; life seemed to cease at the place where the earth let its axle pass, on which it was spinning like a gigantic mill-stone put in movement by a hand of superhuman power. I was afraid, I confess; I crossed myself and prayed to God to return me to the earth, the mother of us all, and in the bosom of which I would doubtless rediscover the mysterious rapidity that ought to take me away from these funereal places.

"The place where I found myself would have been completely plunged in darkness without the crimson reflections of the aurora borealis, which cast a kind of bloody twilight over everything surrounding me. In front of me, the high glaciers of the pole loomed up, whose summits, illuminated by the rays of the Arctic meteor, resembled immense torches lighting the agony of a world. At the foot of the mountains, the darkness gave formidable and grotesque aspects to the rock faces sculpted by the light-ning. Behind me, the colossal black rock next to which the peak of Tenerife and Etna would only have been grains of sand, plunged its base into the void, while its summit was lost in unknown depths. At my feet, all vegetation had ceased, and without the horrible noise of the earth turn-ing on its axle like the flywheel of a steam engine, every-thing would have been death, shadow and silence!

"A profound stupefaction, with which an anxious terror was mingled, had taken possession of me and rendered me motionless. I couldn't take my eyes off the black rock and our poor globe, transpierced by that frightful iron bar, which was rotating with bellowing sounds that were sometimes muffled and sometimes loud enough to give you vertigo

"While I reproached myself for my temerity and my imprudence, and just as I was about to launch myself forth to regain the earth, on which I hoped to recover my primitive velocity, I heard voices and strange laughter, which seemed to be coming from the black rock. I turned my gaze in the direction from which the noises seemed to be coming, and my surprise and fear reached their peak.

"Over the flank of the rock, black giants of some kind were running, as hairy as bears, whose hands seemed to be armed with claws that could fight tigers. On their vast foreheads you could see shining, in letters of fire that seemed to have been engraved by thunderbolts, the words *Legion of Belial no. 6496*. Red flamboyant eyes lit up sinister reflections in their faces, hideously contracted by atrocious laughter. Some of them, lying on the flank of the rock, enveloped by their vast wings, seemed to be sleeping. Others carried vast pitchers of oil that they went to empty over the extremity of the earth's axis. One of them, who appeared to be the leader, looked from time to time at the work his companions were doing, and smiled as he darted glances toward the heavens that chilled the blood in my heart.

"'Well,' said one of the demons to another, 'do you think that we'll have to supervise this stupid planet and turn this annoying handle for much longer? It seems to me that our shift ought to be finished and that the time has come to relieve us? Which legion is on duty next?'

"'Beelzebub's,' replied a voice reminiscent of subterranean thunder.

"'So much the better,' said the first demon. 'I like to see that pride humiliated and transformed from time to time into a turnspit dog. And you, Belial, who came back yesterday from the planet, and have visited it in all directions, inside and out, how many more years do you think we'll have to toil away here and blow on our fingers instead of being able to warm ourselves at our lovely fires of bitumen and sulfur?'

"'In truth,' said the one who had been addressed as Belial, 'I hope that the day of our deliverance is imminent. Everything is worm-eaten, cracked and crumbling on this ridiculous earth. The equator is as worn out as an old barrel-hoop, the tropics are out of kilter, the polar circles are no longer serviceable, they've been patched up so many times. As for the poles, you know as well as I do how much they need immediate repair. Nothing holds together any more, everything's rickety and shaky, everything screeches and cracks—it's enough to make you weep! I was examining the four cardinal points this morning; they're in a deplorable state! North and south, east and west are sometimes so confused that they're no longer recognizable.

"'Word of honor, if I'd fabricated such a stupid machine, I wouldn't brag about it! And then, the weather isn't the only thing at work. Men are helping it out wonderfully! They've dug, pierced and mined the entrails of their globe to such an extent that one of these days everything will disappear into a hole that the Ocean will take charge of filling in. The antipodes will encounter one another by a route of which they've never dreamed. I've visited lands where one walks on a sonorous vault, so profoundly have the sons of Adam disemboweled the poor earth that they've only been condemned to labor.

"'They now have machines that one might believe had been invented by one of us, by means of which they convert a few thousand cubic meters of terrestrial entrails every day into simple smoke. They've succeeded in making nothing out of something! And it's necessary to see how they boast about their *progress!* On the other hand, the volcanoes support us as best they can. I'm sufficiently content with Etna; one of these days it will get rid of part of the coast of Sicily. As for Vesuvius, it's sleeping like a discharged cannon, there's nothing much to hope for in that direction. But talk to me about the Cordilleras! From the Behring Strait to Cape Horn, there's nothing but a sequence of volcanoes that will explode like a mine when the time comes.

"'Anyway, everything's in such disorder on the earth that I encountered winter where I had hoped for spring. The apple-trees and peach-trees are astonished to be waking up from their winter sleep in the midst of snow and ice. The rivers are flowing over the highways and the dejected sun is struggling in vain against the north winds that are splashing the face of a mask of frost in the middle of May! Poor world! We're getting old, and it's high time we unhooked you in order to make urgent repairs!'

"'And how long do you give it before it collapses like a hoopless barrel?' asked one of the demons.

"'That, comrades, depends to some extent on our skill,' said Belial. 'While feigning zeal and simulating obedience, we can hasten the death-throes of the domain of the sons of Adam. For example, one of these days, the equator might perchance break *by accident.* Such things have been seen before, and when they happen to a machine half-broken down, there's no cause for astonishment. So, one of these mornings, while Gabriel, Michael, Ithuriel or another of the feathery plotters of the celestial general staff that have been given to us as overseers is making his customary round, we say to him:

"'*Let Your Excellency not get annoyed and attribute to us the misfortune that has just occurred! The earth has disappeared without our knowing how it happened. Your Lordship will remember that we have often called his attention to numerous defects that have been manifest there for a long time. The equator has burst and the zones, projected by centrifugal force, have flown away like stones hurled by a sling. As for searching for the fragments, Your Courtesy will understand the folly of such a project! We have been charged with the maintenance of the pole, and we have even taken solicitude so far as to galvanize it by means of the Jacobi method to preserve it from rust.*[1]

"'What could whichever of the seraphim is on duty say to that? He'll make his report; we'll sign the document, and all will be said.'

"'The idea of breaking the equator isn't bad,' said a little demon who was blowing on his claws to warm them up, 'but the disaster would be even funnier if we broke the axis of the globe near the pole. That could easily be done without compromising us. I've read in the *Thousand-and-One Nights* that there's a bird called a *pic,*[2] which, when one

---

1 Moritz von Jacobi (1801-1874) invented galvanoplasty, nowadays called electrotyping, in 1838.
2 *Pic* is French for woodpecker, but the reference to the Arabian Nights is enigmatic.

seals its nest by means of an iron plate, goes off to seek a herb that has the property of corroding the hardest metal. Now, by an entirely providential circumstance, I know where to find that herb. What prevents us from applying it one day to the axle of the globe, and one fine morning, *snap!*—off it goes to fly through the fields of chaos at a speed of five hundred million leagues an hour.'

"'My word!' said an old gray-haired demon who had not joined in the conversation until then, occupied as he was with greasing the axle of the pole, 'those are projects that testify to more zeal than experience. In the matter of evil, leave it to humans, and they'll surpass you! Rely on them to disfigure and destroy the domain that God has confided to them. A few centuries from now, this earth, once so beautiful, that Eden where the forests, the plains, the flowers, the waters and the mountains sang the glory of the Creator and the joy of the creature, the earth that God had confided to humans to embellish and fertilize, will be nothing more than the inhospitable and tenebrous abode of a few seals and a few white bears, which will soon disappear, leaving behind nothing but a dismal and icy globe devoid of movement and life.'

"'And how will that come about?' said the little devil who had made the proposal of the *pic* bird's herb.

"'By letting humans, our best and most faithful auxiliaries in the war we're waging on God, go their own way. That biped animal has a certain charm, but does evil gravely, conscientiously and with the calm that accompanies the accomplishment of a duty. What in us is the result of inspiration and instinct is accomplished in humans in the name of a pretended systematic wisdom, which has thus far given rise to nothing but ruins, without opening anyone's eyes.

"'Leave humans alone, I tell you. Already the forests have disappeared from almost all of the surface of Europe, and the moment is not far off when the last tree will fall, wringing a groan from the earth. You know what has become of Asia, almost entirely: the ancient cradle of humankind is, at present, nothing but a torrid and sterile desert, burned by the north wind and the sun, over which the wings of the wind no longer collect even the slightest cloud. I give the Americans three centuries to exhaust the land of Columbus.

"'That done, the evaporations of the Ocean, no longer finding the summits of forests on land to arrest and condense them, will be driven every day toward the poles, where they will go to augment the vast cupola of ice that makes up the polar solitudes. Soon, the Ocean will no longer be anything but a waterless abyss paved with salt, which will dispense with salting the last herring to be fished out of it. On the other hand, the earth, deprived of beneficent rains, open everywhere to the easterly and northerly winds that will blow without encountering obstacles, will become an arid charnel-house in which people will fight over scraps of flesh—and then only will humans love one another, but in a culinary sense. They'll see in their neighbor a steak or a chop, nothing more.'

"'Hurrah!' said the little devil. 'That seems like cause for celebration.'

"'Ah,' said the old demon, with a singular accent of melancholy, addressing the devil child that had interrupted him, 'it's easy to see that you were born yesterday, and that you've never contemplated like us the sublime harmonies of this globe, when it emerged from the right hand of the Creator and the stupid hands and insensate passions of human beings had not yet spoiled its original brightness and marvelous aspect. Those fiery solitudes of Africa where the lion reigns as master; those American savannahs populated by jaguars and wolves; those steppes of northern Asia; those deserts of Mongolia and China where no bird can find a seed to nourish it, were once as many odorous and luminous Edens, full of the songs of waxwings and nightingales. Humans passed that way, and behind them, desolation and death have extended their somber mantle over the work of the Creator. Humans have already used up Asia and Africa; Europe is in the process of going the same way; there remains America, and the isles of Polynesia; let civilization and progress have their way, and soon the earth will be nothing more than a sterile and icy globe, covered in part by salty lakes like those we see on the moon. Like the latter star, it will become a futile reflector, wandering through space, tottering on its ecliptic, disturbed by the augmentation of the weight of the poles, increased by the entire mass of the Ocean turned to ice. That's what humans will end up making of the work of God. You can see that there's no need for our collaboration and our enlightenment.'"

At this point I stopped the narrator in order to make a simple and naïve observation.

"But my dear Jérôme," I said to him, in a fashion that might perhaps have been pierced by a hint of mockery, "in what language were these demons talking, who want us to arrive at such a disagreeable downfall? You're not, so far as I know, versed in cabalistic idioms; how, then, were you able to understand them?"

"In truth, Monsieur, it's quite simple," Jérôme said, propping himself up on his elbow in order to resume his story. "Those demons were speaking the language of the terrestrial paradise—which is to say, the good and pure Flemish of Bruges and Blankenberghe. I've heard it said that scholars have already discovered that circumstance; well, if they need a witness to give their theory further support, I'm ready to affirm that the entire celestial and infernal militia speaks Flemish like you and me."

"It's true, Jérôme, that I can remember having heard that opinion professed."[1]

"It's not an opinion, Monsieur, it's a verity, which is very flattering for Flemings like us; for if the angels and the cloven hooves make use of that language, it's obvious that the good God doesn't employ any other."

"That seems to me to be quite natural, Jérôme; lackeys have to adopt the language of the master. But go on; your story is interesting me greatly."

"I should think so!" said Jérôme. "It interests us all, whether we're Christians, Jews or Turks—all God's creatures, in sum!

"So, after the old devil and the little devil who had just proposed cutting the earth's axle by means of his accursed herb had finished speaking, all their comrades started applauding; some came to shake their claws. Then, all of a

____

1 Author's note: "This discovery, which does honor to the intelligence and patriotism of our scholars, has been published by Monsieur le Conseiller de Grave, in a paper read at the Académie de Bruxelles, and which caused a profound sensation at the time." The reference is to Charles-Joseph de Grave (1735-1803), author of *La République des Champs-Élysées, ou Monde ancien* [The Republic of the Elysian Fields; or, The Ancient World] (1806), which asserts that the Elysium and Enfer of the ancients were, in fact, human societies situated in northern Gaul and the islands of the lower Rhine, where the goddess Circe initiated Odysseus into the Mysteries, and that the Elysians were also Plato's Atlanteans.

sudden, they linked their crooked hands and started dancing an other-worldly jig that would give you gooseflesh just watching it.

"While they were dancing their infernal hop, a clap of thunder was heard, and by the glare of a lightning flash I saw, coming down from the height of the rock, a cavalier so dazzling that one couldn't look at him. At that sight, the devils went back to work and resumed their tools like idle workmen surprised in culpable idleness by the master. The angel was still coming down; he had a sword in his hand that looked as if it were forged from a sheaf of lightning-bolts. With every step that brought him closer to the demons, they trembled in their scorched skins, which was a pleasure to see. Finally, having arrived next to the black companions, he checked that everything was in order, that there was oil in the hub; then, with a gaze that would have eclipsed Saint Elmo's Fire, he said to them in a voice as loud as a trumpet:

"'So I find you idling again, instead of occupying yourselves with the task imposed upon you! Only yesterday your negligence caused two earthquakes, because of the somersaults of the polar axle in its poorly-greased hub. And then, on the planet, people are complaining about the poor condition of a dwelling in which there's a risk of waking up five hundred feet underground; my master is exposed to humiliating pleas to make the necessary repairs to his property! Damnation! If anything similar happens again, I'll comb your coats so thick and thin that in a hundred years from now your hides won't be good for anything but making bagpipes!'

"'To hear is to obey,' said one of the demons humbly. 'However, I'll take the liberty of making the observation to Monseigneur that an accident will happen one of these days that is bound to be blamed on us, even though'—he sighed deeply—'it won't be our fault.'

"'And why will some such accident happen?' asked the angel.

"'It's just, you see, Monseigneur, that this poor planet has been running for a very long time, and you know how many times it's already been patched up. Humans, those wretched creatures that judge the duration of globes by the paltry measure of their own ephemeral existence, and who modestly think themselves the goal and center of creation, believe blissfully nowadays that the series of modifications that the earth has experienced is finished. Because the relief of the continents hasn't varied for six thousand years and the basin of the Ocean has remained the same, they go to sleep in a false security, and no longer believe in the kind of catastrophe that caused the Pyrenees or the Vosges to surge forth from the Ocean in a single night and tore England away from the European continent.

"'However, Monseigneur, a new crisis is brewing; the central fire—the basalt in fusion, which occupies the center of the globe, as you probably know, and which marks two hundred thousand degrees[1] on the pyrometer—has been tormented and agitated for some time, in a fashion that presages a new cataclysm. If I dared emit an opinion, Monseigneur, I'd say that I believe the solid crust to the globe to be too feeble relative to a terrestrial radius of six thousand kilometers. The frailty of that crust, already cracked in many places, will give way one of these days under the pressure of the incandescent mass, the

---

1 Author's note: "The highest temperature that humans can produce by means of their apparatus is four thousand degrees."

temperature of which is capable of reducing an obelisk of Egyptian porphyry to vapor. Now, by comparing, in recent days, the atmospheric pressure exerted on the terrestrial envelope with the upward and expansive force of the central fire, I've obtained results that make me tremble for the future of this poor hovel of a planet which it will soon be necessary to unhook for urgent repairs.'

"While the old demon was explaining his fears regarding the state of the globe to the archangel on duty, the latter was smoothing his beautiful plumes of gilded azure, with a certain complacency. Then, all of a sudden, as if yielding to an envious thought, the blond seraph said to the cloven hoof: 'That's certainly a solicitude for my master's works that might do you credit, if pride, the ancient and eternal sin didn't have a large part in it. You're knowledgeable, my dear fellow, very knowledgeable. What a pity it is that my master's Council of State is deprived of your enlightenment! We faithful angels don't pride ourselves on knowing so much, but . . .'

"'I can see that Your Excellency is about to allege to me the superiority of faith over intelligence; it's an old sermon that I know like the back of my claw. We *former* angels don't think that it's lacking in respect for the Creator to study the thought that presides over his works and the laws of the universe. Today, everything has changed on high; you've replaced the celestial technical college with a conservatory in which the singing isn't always in tune, from what I've heard. . . .'

"'One more word and I'll hit you with three centuries of hard labor in the depths of Etna!' said the angry angel. 'Who has taught you, then, impertinent scorched-skin, to doubt the eternity of my master's work? Your science has served you well; I give you my sincere compliments thereon! So much mathematics to end up making you a turnspit dog—that's flattering! Not another word! And get to work! Know that this globe will still last long enough to enrage you and prove the power of the one who has changed your ethereal light into infernal darkness.'

"After that speech, the angel deployed his wings in order to return to his abode, and he had already given two powerful wing-beats when he changed his mind and, turning toward the accursed, said to him in a calmer tone: 'After all, if there are a few urgent repairs to be made, notify the archangel on duty. Your solicitude will be duly noted.'

"'Monseigneur's orders will be carried out,' said the demon, graciously curbing his hairy and dentellate back, like that which Frans Floris gave the demons of his Last Judgment.[1]

"Beneath the humble and servile speech of the demon one could sense the piercing sting of an irony, to which the angel doubtless paid no attention, for he ascended toward heaven again after having given a further order to his slaves to see to their work.

"As soon as the last luminous trace accompanying the flight of the angel like a fiery wake had disappeared, the black workmen resumed their infernal dance, and I took advantage of their distraction to regain the earth, where I soon sensed that I had recovered my marvelous rapidity, by means of which it seemed to me that I could have defied the flock of demons."

---

1 Frans Floris (1517-1570) was a Flemish painter associated with the Renaissance movement of Romanism. His painting of the Last Judgment, currently in the Vienna Kunsthistorisches Museum, has a demon in the foreground with a strange jaggedly-ridged spine.

"But do you realize," I said to the fisherman, "that you've taken a great responsibility on yourself by not revealing the frightful plot that you've overheard?"

"And how could I have done that? A single movement might have revealed my presence, and God knows what my fate would have been in the claws of that accursed lot! And yet, I'm reproaching myself now for not having had the courage. It seems to me that, at any moment, our poor earth might blow up like a bomb or sink like an anchor whose cable has been cut. I had horrible dreams last night! From now on, my life is poisoned; I'll no longer be able to go to bed at night without wondering whether I'll wake up in that thick darkness, in the middle of which the rock of the pole rises up. And to think that there's no remedy for it, no means of preventing the peril or of avoiding it! Oh, Monsieur, it will drive me mad!"

"It would indeed be enough to trouble one's reason, my dear Jérôme, if what you told me just now was anything but the feverish dream of a delirious mind."

"You, too, Monsieur! You think I've lost my mind! But if anything could make me lose it, it would doubtless be these attestations from the captains of three ships in harbor in the Gulf of Finland, which prove that at seven o'clock this morning they saw and talked to me and gave me letters for Antwerp and Ostend; there are also certificates signed by the mariners of the Great Belt in the Baltic Sea, which declare that I, Jérôme Axël, have taken cognizance this morning of their cargo, the place of their destination, the names of their ships and those of their owners. Look at these letters and documents, and dare to say after that that I'm mad!"

While speaking thus, Jérôme took a packet of letters from the pocket of his overcoat, which I red with a profound terror. Those attestations were in order, and then, the honest fisherman would have been incapable of lying, and even less of forging such documents.

"I don't understand anything of your adventure, my good Jérôme," I said, in a faint voice, "but tell me how you got out of that terrible peril, and how you arrived here safe and sound."

"This is how, Monsieur: at the moment when I reached the earth I threw myself on my knees to thank God for having saved me from a danger compared with which ten shipwrecks would have been nothing for me. A pale twilight was illuminating the frightful bare and icy rocks that surrounded me. I marched southwards; I traversed the bitter solitudes of the Samoyeds, the Tax, the Obi and a host of rivers unknown to our geographers. I went along the mouths of the Yenisei, the Gulf of Gdansk, that of the Ob and that of the Kola; then, turning westwards, I traversed the Urals to the source of the Petchora, where I fell down, exhausted by all the emotions that had shaken me so rudely since my departure from Blankenberghe, where my wife must have been very worried about my absence.

"At sunrise, I resumed my route, leaving Archangel to the right and still bearing westwards. A few minutes later I arrived in Saint Petersburg, where I had breakfast with the two francs I had left. I would dearly have liked to see that city, but in my situation that was impossible. Any step I took transported me considerable distances. I quit the capital of Russia going along the gulf of Finland. In a few minutes I reached the shore of the Baltic. I crossed the Vistula, the Oder, the Elbe and the Rhine, where I paused for a few minutes to admire the beauty of that noble river, which bears burgs and castles like a crown.

"While I was contemplating the ruined towers, perched on the summits of mountains like watchmen on the yard-arms, a young man in a green cap with a sack on his back and a long pipe in his hand joined me and asked, with the familiarity that it so rapidly established on the highways between people who don't know one another, where I was coming from and where I was going.

"'I'm coming from Cape Severovostoschnoï, comrade,' I said to him, smiling.

"'And where the devil did you find that cape on the Rhine, friend?

"'I found it where it is, which is to say, on the seventy-ninth degree of north latitude and the hundredth of longitude. It forms the northern extremity of the earth. Even the white bears don't go out without gloves there, so pleasant is the climate.'

"'And how long have you been *en route*, comrade?'

"'In truth, nearly two hours. That makes fifteen hundred leagues an hour.'

"'Ah!' sad the German, scanning me attentively from head to foot, but especially the feet. Then he drew closer and said to me, in a low voice: 'You found *them* in the White Sea no doubt, for it's there that Peter Schlemihl, the man who sold his shadow to the Devil, lost them!'[1]

"In my turn I looked at the German to see whether he was making fun of me; but he went on, with the same mystery: 'What conditions has Old Nick put upon you in

---

1 The reference is to the classic Faustian fantasy *Peter Schelmihls wundersame Geschichte* (1814; translated as *Peter Schlemihl, or The Shadowless Man*) by the exiled French aristocrat Adalbert von Chamisso.

order to let go of that marvelous talisman?' You know, Monsieur, that Old Nick is an English term, which means Satan.

"'My friend,' I said to the stranger, 'give me the pleasure of talking to me as a Christian; I don't understand oracles and mysteries.'

"'Damn it!' said the German. 'It seems to me that I'm making myself clear. You've come from the northern extremity of Asia to Mayence in two hours. Now tell me if there's any shoemaker in the world, except the Devil, who can provide a man with footwear to travel in that fashion? You have the famous seven league boots, of the ogre killed by Pettit Poucet. After the latter's death the Devil bought them back, but they were stolen from him by Peter Schlemihl, who drowned in the White Sea, which he thought he could traverse in a single leap, thinking that it was the Gulf of Kandalask, which is further to the north. In any case, I know your boots; my grandfather, who had seen them, gave me their description several times. And you can think yourself lucky if your black bootmaker doesn't only take for payment the salvation of your soul.'

"As the German was speaking a cold sweat inundated my limbs; my eyes misted over; my teeth were chattering like a sail whipped by a hurricane; I thought for a moment that I could see a ferocious gleam in the German's eye that froze my blood; his red beard seemed to be ablaze! Without being able to explain my dread, I drew away abruptly from the stranger, who seemed to me to be all the more suspect because he affected to keep his hands constantly in the vast pockets of his trousers.

"I took two steps, and found myself alone again on the bank of the Rhine, prey to a thousand strange thoughts.

My accursed boots seemed to be burning my feet. The velocity that seemed marvelous to me at first now frightened me. It seemed that an infernal and invisible hand was pushing me. However, the sight of the bell-tower of Bruges rendered me a little courage, and I soon found myself transported to the door of my dwelling, where my wife, prey to mortal anguish, had been waiting for me since the previous day. The unfortunate woman hadn't been to bed all night.

"'Take off these boots, these accursed boots!' I shouted at my wife, letting myself fall into a chair. 'Get them off me, and may I never see them again as long as I live!'

"Without saying a word, my wife took my boots off, and I threw myself on my bed, where it appears that the memory of what has happened to me since yesterday has made me say things that my neighbors have taken for delirium.

"That's my story, Monsieur. And now, on your salvation, swear to me that, when you gave me those fatal boots, you were unaware of their power and their infernal virtue?"

"On my soul I swear it, Jérôme," I said, ardently, "and I'll be even more sincere; if I'd known their occult power, I assure you that I'd have kept them for myself. For a long time, I've dreamed of making a tour of the world in an economical manner. But where are these magic boots that the ogre, Petit Poucet, Peter Schlemihl and you have each worn in your turn without wearing them out?"

"They've doubtless gone back whence they came," said the fisherman's wife, who came back in at that moment. "I've just thrown them out of the window, and a sort of beggar that I don't know fell upon them as on a long-awaited prey. Then he put them on in the middle of the street, looking at me with a kind of smile that reeked of sulfur. A second later, the mendicant had disappeared."

"Perhaps you were in too much of a hurry," I said to the fisherman's wife. "I would have been very curious to try them out."

"May Heaven preserve you from that, Monsieur," said Jérôme, "for I sense that the memory of what I've seen by that fatal means will kill me."

In fact, poor Jérôme, still preoccupied with the malice of the demons charged with the maintenance of the pole, died a few days later, in a fit of delirium, during which he wanted to oppose the attempts of black workmen occupied in corroding the axle of the globe by means of the herb known to the *pic* bird.

And now, who can tell whether Jérôme was mad? The captains who arrived from the Gulf of Finland four or five months after his death have declared that the letters found in the fisherman's hands were authentic, and that they had given them five months previously to a man who affirmed that he had departed two hours before from the northern extremity of Asia, and who wanted to get back to Blankenberghe before dinner time, in order not to worry his wife.

A NOCTURNAL VISIT

THE proverb "No one is a prophet in his own country" can be applied to the monuments and architectonic rarities of a country as well as the people. The habit of living side-by-side with the marvels of art or nature must singularly blunt the admiration that they inspire in those who see them for the first time. Thus, we can understand perfectly the bewilderment of the Arabs of the desert at the sight of the intrepid tourists who brave the simoom, the plague, thieves, privations and sunstroke to come and admire the mountains of rubble beneath which the Pharaohs of Memphis went to savor an eternal repose and youth that they had sought in vain during their lives. On seeing our scholars and artists measuring and drawing the great sphinxes of pink granite which, extending their paws in the sun, gaze at the Orient with their eyes of stone as if they were waiting for some new Sesostris; on seeing the caravans of Englishmen, fully impregnated with British ennui, having their dinner served on the knees of some Nubian god—a mysterious colossus half-buried in the vast shroud of the desert sands—the Egyptian cicerones have doubtless asked themselves more than once what there is in those ruins that can interest Europeans so much that they risk being baked by the sun, robbed by Arabs or eaten by the crocodiles of the Nile, those ancient gods of Egypt that still levy such a heavy tithe upon their former worshipers.

The infatuation of a few individuals, and the publication of a few fashionable guides, have sufficed in England to make the Rhine and its banks all the rage. People have come to demand legends or exciting stories of every ruin of the Taunus or the Schwartzwald, as if the Ardennes, that harsh and poetic land, did not bear on the front of each of its manors, blackened by fire or breached by battering-rams and cannons, a sad or glorious legend. But these things go in such a fashion that the Germans know very little about the banks of their Old Father Rhine, all the ruins of which have been visited by the least English tourist, whereas, on the other hand, the English address themselves to German travelers in order to know Scotland.

And are not we ourselves a little bit English in this regard? We have our Belgian Rhine, the Meuse, whose waves have sometimes been reddened by the reflections of conflagration, and sometimes by the blood that has come to mingle with its waters. From Givet to Maestricht, how many ruins, manors and châteaux there are whose names are attached to our ardent national struggles! Every tower that mirrors its mutilated head, deprived of its crown of crenellations, in the waters of the river would have strange things to tell us if we knew how to interrogate it. But as more vanity enters into tourism than intelligent curiosity, and as it is primarily a matter of making the figure of one's fortune known by the expenses of a distant voyage, all of our burgers, bankers and retired businessmen, as soon as spring arrives, shut themselves up in a noisy post-chaise and depart, furnished with a guide to Italy, for the eternal city.

The bourgeois and the English have spoiled Italy; they have left on that old land of Caesars and Michelangelo a trail of commercial prosaicism like the tracks of slime that slugs leave on walls. The bourgeois and the English are to be found in every corner of Rome, the former astonished that the Coliseum has not been demolished in order to build nice houses that would make the Pope six per cent on his money, the latter peering at the Pantheon of Agrippa that Michelangelo has thrown three hundred feet into the air and murmuring, in a bored fashion: "Very nice. Very pretty." After a fortnight of tedium, when he believes that he has satisfied the exigencies of fashionable tourism, the bourgeois or the Englishman goes home, summarizing the impressions of his voyage, the former declaring that Rome is a city in dire need of repair and the latter astonished that the Romans live in such complete ignorance of pigeon pie, rump steak and Barclay Stout.[1]

But now we're a long way from our subject, and the legend that we want to recount to you.

Without going very far from Brussels, when the season comes in which the hawthorn perfumes the by-ways and the voice of a bird twitters in every briar-patch, one can, in our opinion, undertake charming artistic and romantic excursions around the capital. It is sufficient for that to equip oneself with a few cigars and to set forth for Léau,

------

1 "Russian Imperial Stout," first brewed by Barclay Perkins in 1781, more recently brewed by Courage under its own brand name, but acquired by Wells & Young in 2006.

Leefdael, Gasbeek, Villers, the abbey of Aulne, Groenendael, Beersel, etc., etc.

Each of those localities, abbeys, châteaux and ruins, we can declare, has its legend, sometimes somber and almost always poetic. It seems that the memories of another age no longer have any dwelling today but those crumbling walls, those fissured towers, those manors that pellitory and wallflowers cover with a mantle of verdure and blossoms as if to hide the insults of time and those, even more terrible, of human passions.

Among all those ruins, the Château de Beersel is one of the most remarkable.[1] The wind and the rain have, especially in the last twenty years, caused frightful ravages in that formidable manor, which still raises toward the sky its three towers, whose walls are no less than seven feet thick. Around the château there is a dried-up moat, which is covered every spring by an odorous snow of daisies and myosotis. Two beams and a few planks are all that remain of the bridge that once resonated under the feet of men-at-arms and warhorses. Above the postern constellated with nails the opening can be seen from which the heavy iron portcullis once descended.

The towers are linked by a circular rampart that was once covered and crenellated, from behind which the arrows and catapult-stones departed in order to pierce heavy suits of armor and coats of mail. Today, that rampart is uncovered and overlooks the courtyard of the château, where thick grass grows vigorously. The three towers, fissured as if struck by lightning, astonish by their aspect of

---

1 The fourteenth-century Beersel Castle—Kasteel van Beersel in Dutch—was "restored" in the 1920s and is now a routine tourist attraction.

grandeur and strength. They are mountains of stone, in each plane of which one could sculpt a house. The summit of the keep, deprived of its diadem of white battlements, bears a crest of saplings sown by the birds, which threaten to become tall poplars or magnificent elms. The spiral staircases, now crumbled, obstruct the interior of the towers; the windows lashed by the wind awaken a host of sonorous echoes in all the corners of the manor. The vast rooms have no other vault than the blue azure of the sky.

In sum, the Château of Beersel realizes, in the most complete fashion, the type-specimen of those old feudal remains destined to be the theater of strange events.

It would be rather curious to investigate why the fantastic only finds its normal environment in the midst of the ruins of an ardent, passionate and brutal past, such as the Middle Ages were. The natural frame of any drama of the afterlife is a crumbling keep in which the wind weeps with plaintive voices and which, once night has fallen, the shadows only populate with indecisive forms, unusual noises and sinister gleams, while outside, in the pure and calm nocturnal air, the birds of darkness describe their diabolical spirals, uttering lamentable cries that harmonize marvelously with everything that surrounds them.

Instead of that, set a fantastic drama in a modern château, built in the Italian style, with its straight and pure architectural lines, and you will lack one of the essential conditions of the drama—which is to say, the combination of grandeur and mystery that gives all those old witnesses of an age of blood and violence the cachet that nothing can replace.

There is no one, we believe, even a notary, a banker or the proprietor of a cheap lodging-house—all people little inclined to the marvelous—who has not wanted at least once in life to witness one of the mysterious resurrections that are sometimes accomplished in ruins that are so picturesque when the sun is risen but which the wing of night populates with so many moving terrors. Everyone has desired—while fearful of it—to witness one of the strange discussions that the guests of the sepulcher hold in places dedicated to their silence.

One would like to see the old portraits descend from their frames, the gigantic sphinxes of fireplaces stretch out their formidable claws, uttering a sonorous yawn, the dusty old saints and stone barons quit their niches and their sepulchral stones to come, in a ray of moonlight, to stroll along the crumbling ramparts or meditated in the angle of some window traversed by the osprey and the owl, the natural commensals of all these tenebrous affairs. If the fantastic has such irritating charms on imaginations devoted to the positive things of life, what power of attraction must it exert on poetic, impassioned, feverish natures, friends of the marvelous, who have desired twenty times over the good fortune Don Juan had in enabling the old commander to descend from his marble tomb to come to sup with him?

Ten years ago, I found myself in all the conditions required to be the hero of an apparition. I know not what fantasy, in which the idleness of a lazzarone and the dreamy contemplation of the poet played a large part, had drawn me to Beersel in order to complete my studies of the English poets there. It was an admirable place to read Byron and the poetic legends of Walter Scott. One can only fully understand Lara, Manfred and the Lady of the Lake in those solitudes. My days were spent shooting swallows and jays, reading Byron, smoking and sleeping under the old oaks of the avenue that runs alongside the château to the right.

The vast courtyard of the manor, cleared of stables, the chapels and the commons destined for men-at-arms and valets, is no more today than a large circular space in which vigorous grass grows, mingled with briars and brambles. The black arches of the subterrains, deprived of their doors, stand out sharply against the red and brown hues of the towers that dominate them. In the daytime, a few goats and pigs wander at liberty in the château, which, once the postern is closed, has no exit and could still withstand a routine assault.

I spent entire days in the manor, amusing myself shooting, from the top of the ramparts, the jays and crows that inhabited the oaks of the avenue. Once or twice I lingered in the great hall of the southern tower, the only one that possessed a first-floor room whose vault had not collapsed under the rain. Several times I had formed the plan of spending the night there in the company of my dog, a fine black spaniel with a silky coat, who waged rude war on the rats that were the veritable proprietors of the beautiful ruin, which the Duke of Aremberg could save with a few crumbs of his immense income.

Finally, one day, I came to take possession of the château; I brought a mattress that, placed in the embrasure of a window, six feet wide, made me a kind of alcove, sufficiently comfortable. Then, after having equipped myself with an armful of dead wood, two candles and a lighter, I went bravely to install myself in the large reception room, of which the bats did me the honors with a flutter of wings that did not announce anything good.

Toward nine o'clock, the last rays of the setting sun covered the damp walls of the room with a golden dust; I started a blaze in the vast fireplace, which soon illuminated the whole room and chased the shadows from the least corners. After having closed the doors to the ramparts and those that led to the collapsed second floor, I went to lie down on my mattress.

The sounds in the village gradually died away, and nothing could any longer be heard but the nocturnal breeze moaning in the high treetops. Sometimes, a bat, frightened by the bright light of my fire, came to traverse the room, drawing muffled growls from Puck, who did not understand what it was that I found agreeable in that new abode, where the wind came in through the windows with night-birds, and where caravans of rats held their nocturnal assizes.

Soon, the most complete silence reigned everywhere, and except for the occasional shutter banging in the wind, which woke up the echoes of the manor, no sound reached me.

Puck had bravely taken possession of my mattress, and had not taken long to discover the sleep of the just, fatigued by beating the meadows and the bushes throughout a long summer day. As for me, in spite of my preoccupations, my fears and my desire to see some formidable mystery accomplished before my eyes, sleep began to gain on me, and while reading the incantation scene in *Manfred*, I sensed, as Villon puts it, the windbreaks of my eyes closing. Before yielding entirely to sleep, however, I went to stoke up my fire, and I threw a few faggots thereon that promised me at least two hours of the bright light that, it is said, causes vagabonds to flee from tombs. Then, after my last round of the room, I went to lie down, taking care to place my double-barreled shotgun, methodically loaded with lead shot, to whose virtue I attached the greatest faith, within arm's reach.

It is necessary to say everything; I did not sleep soundly; my light, feverish somnolence represented to me all the terrible scenes with which stupid reading had larded my head. All the horrors of Ann Radcliffe and *Melmoth* came to obsess me. Sometimes, I seemed to see the wall opening up to let nameless, terribly absurd entities pass. Sometimes I saw the abominable witches of the heath of Glamis coming to do their infernal cooking, from which Macbeth's destiny emerged, before my eyes. Then the silence was populated by mysterious voices and bizarre forms that called to one another and replied; or else I saw at my feet my honest Puck swell up and grow like Faust's black barbet, to fill the entire room. All possible nightmares whipped my brain, and when I woke up, I felt exhausted, as if my body had followed my mind in the vagabond cycle of its fantastic course.

The sight of Puck sleeping peacefully refreshed my blood. *In fact*, I thought, *why should I be any less tranquil than that animal; I haven't killed Banquo or anyone else; I haven't made any pact with Satan, and as for the nonsense that populates my mind, it's at moments like this that I realize how far a spaniel is above a Christian who has furnished his head with the stupidities of novelists and poets.*

My mind was reasoning, but that reasoning didn't calm my blood, enfevered by all the mysterious obsessions of silence, memories and the place where I was.

I got up, and went to the window. The night was calm and beautiful; the moon, sitting on opaline clouds, was leading the nocturnal choir of the stars, which seemed to be passing beneath the feet of God, murmuring a hymn to his grandeur and power. The oaks and poplars curbed their heads as if to salute that magnificent spectacle.

That sight reanimated me completely, and I believe that at that moment, I could have braved the nine circles of Dante's horrors.

I went to lie down again, reassured and tranquil, and did not take long to fall asleep, promising myself to laugh the next day at my nocturnal terrors devoid of any object.

I had been asleep for about an hour when I was abruptly woken up by the growling and movements of Puck, who was standing up on the bed, his nose turned toward one of the doors that led to the rampart, and which, deprived of bolts, opened inwards at a simple shove. I thought at first that Puck had been woken up by some rat, but his persistence in gazing and growling at the door to the rampart made me anxious. I calmed him down, and listened with the contention of hearing that perceived the fall of a leaf or the movement of an insect in the silence of the night.

A slow and muted sound, like that of footsteps on grass, was audible.

All the terrors that had assailed my mind an hour before came back in a host, magnified this time by a certainty that I could not deny, and which was doubtless about to render me spectator to some tenebrous mystery.

From one minute to the next the sound of footsteps became increasingly more distinct. I held Puck by the head and took care to grip his muzzle between my hands in order to stifle his growling, which might have prevented me from hearing the sounds coming from outside. Suddenly, the footfalls stopped, and the door to the rampart resounded with a dull blow, followed by a singular scraping.

At that sound, Puck disengaged himself violently from my hands and launched himself toward the door, barking furiously. Then, suddenly coming back, he took refuge between my legs, tail lowered, as if the first impulse of his instinct had misled him as to the veritable nature of the approaching enemy.

That fear on the part of my dog caused a whole world of ideas to cross my mind. Was I about to come face to face with one of the guests of the tomb? Was I about to witness some congress similar to the one that Faust saw on the summit of the Brocken? Or had the old Barons Van Witthem, the ancient lords of the manor, come to weep over their towers, destroyed by the decadence of their lineage? The most reasonable of those suppositions was made to inspire vertigo; the least frightening was of a nature to terrify the best-tempered brain.

The noise at the door continued; the friction became increasingly urgent. Soon, I saw the door shaking. As rapid as thought, I picked up my rifle, and waited with horrible heartbeats for the conclusion of the adventure. At the sight of the rifle, and the sound of the hammers being cocked, Puck regained courage and gave voice.

Finally, the door opened slowly, in the midst of Puck's muffled growling as he pressed himself ever more closely against me. I saw—or, rather, glimpsed—a somber mass in the gap in he doorway, and without waiting any longer I fired a shot in that direction, the detonation of which,

reverberated by the echoes of rooms and the spiral staircases of the towers, woke up legions of ospreys, which
took flight with a sinister flutter of wings.

The sound of my gunshot had not been loud enough,
however, that I could not hear, through the sonorous vi-
bration of the air, a piercing cry like that of a wounded
man. Puck, to whom the gunshot had returned his hunting instincts, barked loudly enough to wake the dead.

For myself, without any thought, like an automaton,
I reloaded my empty barrel, and, armed again, I awaited
events, if not with calm, at least with a stupid resolution.

Three quarters of an hour went by, during which I was
able to count my pulse-beats. Puck had gone to the door
of the rampart and sniffed violently, while scratching the
ground and turning his head from time to time toward me,
as if to summon me and tell me to follow him. Standing in
my embrasure, however, I did not budge any more than a
boundary-stone. All my faculties were converted into one:
hearing. And it seemed to me that I could hear precipitate
footsteps in the neighboring tower, which gradually died
away in the distance.

Finally, dawn blanched the sky and the first rays of the
rising sun gilded the summits of the towers. The awakened
birds chattered in the foliage, and all of nature seemed
to be emerging from its slumber. I breathed out, as if a
mountain had been lifted from my breast. In that beautiful
and joyous morning light, nothing deadly and evil could
be encountered. The reign of darkness was ended, and
with it that of the things that belonged to it.

Puck was still summoning me toward the door of the
rampart; this time, I went resolutely. On opening it, however, I saw the white stone threshold stained with blood.

Stupefied by that sight, I stood there as if petrified. It was not a dream of my imagination that had haunted me, and what I had glimpsed opening the door was not a phantom evoked by my mind. Those traces of blood were quite fresh, palpable, and real; my lead had hit someone, or something.

The sun rose higher in the sky. The village woke up with the cock's crow; I heard carts creaking in the distance in the ruts of the local by-roads. It was daylight! For me, everything was in that word. I followed Puck, who made me traverse the rampart, and, having arrived at the tower to the right of the postern, I saw more traces of blood on the gray steps of the stone spiral. Those traces disappeared momentarily at the base of the tower, but going on, guided by Puck, I found them again at the entrance to a subterrain, where they disappeared into the damp earth.

In all of that there was some mystery that I could not comprehend. My thoughts, calmed by the morning air, now rejected disdainfully the somber beliefs and superstitious terrors that I had refrained from doubting amid the silence of the night. That blood did not belong to a phantom, and unless I had wounded a gnome or broken the wing of a djinni I could not explain that proof of the presence of a material being.

I was plunged in those thoughts when urgent blows caused the postern to resound. I went to open it, and a young herdsman came in without saying a word and ran toward the subterrain. Puck followed him ardently, and after a few minutes I saw them both coming back, driving before them a large black hog whose bloody head bore the traces of my lead shot.

"Look, Monsieur," the child said to me, whipping the pig with great blows of a switch, "this brigand has scratched his muzzle, doubtless falling down some stairway. Yesterday, I couldn't find him to bring him home—fortunately, my father doesn't know anything about it."

Everything was explained—and yet, in spite of that trivial denouement of my night in the Château de Beersel, I know people who have seen things there that still await an explanation.

Perhaps I shall tell you one of these days the bizarre legend of the man in the green hat.

THE DEATH OF GUILLAUME D'AREMBERG DE LA MARCK, KNOWN AS THE WILD BOAR OF THE ARDENNES

I

IT is a marvelous thing to see the facility with which errors invade human intelligence, which seems, by virtue of its propensity to accumulate lies, to be an ingrate and infertile terrain in which the absurd germinates and grows with an unusual vigor, while the truth needs hard and constant labor in order to develop, and often, meager as it is, remains devoid of result.

For several years, especially, a historical school has been founded in those crypts of the press known as *feuilletons* that threatens to give a thread to twist to future Saumaises.[1] Walter Scott, may God preserve him, was the first who, with neither modesty not dread, came to graft pastiche and fantasy on to the grave and severe trunk of history, which was thus stifled beneath the luxurious and

---

1 The reference is to the French classical scholar Claude Saumaise (1588-1653), who signed his Latin works Claudius Salmasius.

florid lianas of his poetic imagination. Soon, a host of imitators, rushing in the tracks of the Scottish novelist, arranged the annals of every people so fully and so well that they were soon able, like Sganarelle, to reply to astonished simpletons: "We have changed all that."[1]

An unprecedented disorder, a diluvian confusion, a tenebrous and inextricable chaos was the consequence of that new historical system in which people sought in vain to rediscover the primitive lineaments of their national physiognomy. The truth no longer being anything more than an accessory, and the drama having become the principal thing, people did not concern themselves with facts, dates, virtues or vices. They went further, in accordance with the demands of the drama, the novel or the *feuilleton*, crime was canonized, virtue calumniated, and as if the history of human folly and baseness did not offer a sufficiently rich and lush field to the imagination, monstrous reputations were rehabilitated that history had stamped with a deal of reprobation and scorn.

People strove to prove that Nero was worthy of all the Prix Monthyons of ancient Rome, that Caligula, Richard III, Don Pedro of Castile, Philippe II and the worthy Monsieur Robespierre were honest men to whom history owed expiatory monuments. The reverse was done with regard of the virtuous, who were very astonished to find themselves one morning the object of sharp and heated accusations. The chaste and cold Mary Tudor became a kind of Northern Messalina. What saintly and modest crowns have the hands of poets not snatched away from

---

1 Sganarelle is a name derived from an Italian word meaning "descale"—disillusion, in the metaphorically sense of scales falling from the eyes—ironically given to several characters by Molière.

the most chaste heads? With what muddy calumnies have innocent robes not been splashed, while a nimbus of gold has been cast around the heads of names pilloried by history? Profound wretchedness, or corruption even more profound, that does not even respect the heritage of the illustrious dead: the good renown of virtue and chastity for women, that of courage and loyalty for men!

We were able to see some little time ago in our theaters the moral rehabilitation of one of the jackals that history shows us ever hasty to fell victims beneath the tiger's claw, to shove the proscribed beneath the executioner's axe or noose: Vargas, the ferocious bloodhound of the Duc d'Albe has been depicted for us as a holy martyr to patriotism. A man has had the courage to clean up that bloody figure, to absolve that tenebrous soul.[1]

Then came other poets, other writers, who have undertaken tasks no less arduous. Some, rummaging in the most noxious sewers of the eighteenth century—that century of corruption and satanic vices—have exhumed the frightful memory of the Marquis de Sade, to try to ennoble him and have him absolved by literary talent. Then came the apotheosis of Madame de Brinvilliers, Robespierre, Jean Châtel, etc., etc., whom our novelists and poets have presented by turns to the astonished century as the victims of an epoch that did not have the stature of those giants of passion, intelligence or genius.

And that is your doing, Walter Scott! Those are the fruits of your writing, O great poet of Abbotsford! It is through the breach that you made in history that all these

---

1 The reference is to *Le Bourgeois de Gand* (1838) by Hippolyte Romand, one copy of which is mistakenly attributed to Joly by Google Books.

impious iconoclasts have introduced themselves who are rushing insanely around the sacred pantheon of peoples, profaning or crowning, in accordance with the needs of their momentary works, those ancient renowns of grandeur or ruination! That is what has been produced by a great but deadly example, with the consequence that today, astonished and confused nations no longer know to whom to award triumphs or on whom to inflict ignominy.

And when we cast our gaze upon our literary past, a past as temporary as our future, we sense that we have not remained pure of historical calumnies, that we too have sometimes, in "the interests of drama," as one puts it nowadays, polluted some fine and noble name, embellished or ornamented some somber or bloody memory. We want, therefore, today, O great master, to pay our debt to the truth by showing in his true colors the last moments of a man that you sacrificed, "in the interests of drama," charged with your anathemas, without a regret, without a tear for his unfortunate and pitiful end.

Please forgive us for that long digression, that pompous peristyle to a mediocre monument, but we needed to justify our reproaches and explain the motive that causes us to undertake, today, the recounting of an incident that error has popularized, but which is not known in its true light: we want to talk about the last moments of Guillaume de la Marck, known as the Wild Boar of the Ardennes, whose somber figure fills a magnificent episode in one of the finest novels of Water Scott, *Quentin Durward*.[1]

---

1 The picture of "William de La Marck" offered by Scott, who employed him as the villain of *Quentin Durward*, does indeed only pay lip service to historical events, but it is not obvious that Joly's rival account is much less fanciful, and this claim is somewhat tongue-in-cheek.

Few men have been more severely treated by history than that bold military leader, whose name resounds in the chroniclers of the fifteenth century like a knell of death and terror. His ferocious bravery, his instincts of murder and pillage, his savage energy, his cruel vengeances, his bitter thirst for riches and sensuality, judged from the viewpoint of our present mores, certainly deserve to be delivered to the execration of posterity; but if one places oneself mentally in the milieu of the fifteenth century, so full of bloody and furious battles, pitiless vengeances, wars in which victors and vanquished soiled themselves in turn with the same horrors, wallowed in the same mire, in which the executioner came at the end of every battle as a gleaner for the gibbet or the scaffold; when treaties were, for the Burgundians or the French, nothing but a trap in which each party sought to ensnare the other; in which a young man, Louis de Bourbon, uniting on his head at nineteen years of age both temporal and spiritual power, scandalized and wounded a nation by his shameful debauchery and insolent despotism—if, as we say, one places oneself at that point of view, the only one from which judgment can sanely be passed on the interesting fraction of the Middle Ages that ended with the peace of Arras, one will have a very different idea of the formidable Liègois mercenary, whose death was a crime, committed, like so many others in that epoch, to avenge another.

The peace of Arras had just been signed, on 12 December 1482,[1] between two champions equally fatigued

1 The treaty of 1482 put a temporary end to the conflict between the French King Louis XI and Maximilian, the Hapsburg husband of Marie de Bourgogne, both of whom were eager to acquire the Burgundian provinces in France that she had inherited; her death earlier that year had created a problem of inheritance, Maximilian being specifically excluded under the terms of his marriage contract.

by a long and cruel war. Louis XI, from the bosom of his deathbed, finally enjoyed the realization of his life's work: the abasement of the house of Bourgogne, which his cold and implacable hatred had pursued all the way to the children of the daughter of Charles the Bold. France and exhausted Belgium counted their wounds and their ruins. Liège, the audacious city whose pride was curbed without ever breaking, still bloody from the long struggle, obeyed the iron hands of Guillaume de la Marck, who came to fray for his son Jean a bloody path to the double crown of the proud commune.

Rid of his principal enemy, Louis de Valois, who had always been a faithful, although secret, ally of Guillaume de la Marck, Maximilien thought that the moment had come to take his revenge for the sad and cruel end of his uncle, Louis de Bourbon. Abandoned to his own forces, which were negligible compared with Maximilien's, the Wild Boar of the Ardennes sensed that the moment was approaching when he would have to render severe account, and in which many voices would demand of him blood for blood, vengeance for vengeance.

After a few furious battles in which he lost the greater part of his ferocious young boars, recruited on the streets of Paris among the vagrants and cut-throats, mercenaries and thieves who appear at the end of any long war like vultures after a battle; after a few desperate but futile efforts, Guillaume de la Marck shut himself away in Liège, from which, after a siege of several weeks, he emerged safe and sound, taking twenty thousand gold écus and the pledge of the seigneurie of Boullon that he was able to combine with the rich seigneurie of Franchimont, which he had obtained previously from the chapter of Liège.

Still borne to follow the inclination of his imagination, Walter Scott, under the simple title of "The Wild Boar of the Ardennes," given by the chroniclers to Guillaume d'Aremberg, felt obliged to give the latter a vague resemblance to the animal who blind impetuosity and indomitable courage he was the incarnation; and if our memory is not mistaken, the Scottish poet went so far as to give him ivory tusks, doubtless to heighten the valor of the young Briton under whose claymore he caused the valiant mercenary to fall.[1]

Enclosed in his Château d'Aigremont, to which he had retired with the debris of his infernal band, whose red doublets, ornamented by a black boar on the sleeve, cast terror into the hearts of the bravest, de la Marck only rarely permitted himself those beloved excursions in which he fell into the middle of the plains of Brabant, as rapid and as devastating as a torrent. Still strong in spite of his age, he cursed like an old soldier at being subjected to that claustral existence, which was as suited to his predatory appetites as a crown of flowers to a Milanese morion. The memory of the murder at Grivegnée, in which his benefactor had fallen at his feet, his head split by a battle-axe, obsessed him; he needed, in order for him to set aside his remorse or regret, the hot and virile emotions of battle, in which the clash of swords galvanizes a man and the presence of danger makes all other emotions fall silent. His pleasures were hunting and the education of his daughter, an angel fallen with her robe of innocence into the midst of that pandemonium, ignorant of her father's bloody and fatal renown.

While the terrible mercenary reposed in his aerie of

____

1 It is not, in fact, Quentin who kills William de la Marck in Scott's novel.

Aigremont, after repairing its formidable walls, destroyed by Louis de Bourbon in 1474—a bloody affront for which Guillaume de la Marck had subsequently taken an implacable vengeance—and while the region of Liège bandaged its wounds, still gasping from the last ten years, the bloodiest in its history, Jean de Horne, Louis de Bourbon's successor, had not abandoned the idea of one day avenging on Guillaume de la Marck the crushing and insolent domination that the latter had exerted for such a long time in the territory of Liège. To attack in breach of faith of the peace treaties of 22 May 1483, in an invincible citadel, the man to whom he had sworn peace and good faith on the Holy Evangelists was, for Jean de Horne, too audacious an enterprise, and too favorable to the enemy he wanted to defeat. As, in addition, the Wild Boar had numerous friends among the people and could count on the scattered debris of his old bands, whom peace had reduced to repose, and who were only waiting a signal and the sight of a golden gonfaron of Aremberg with a bloody boar's-head for a crest to recommence their career of murder and pillage, the prudent bishop thought of obtaining by cunning what he could not obtain by overt force.

The bishop had two brothers, the Comte de Horne and the Sire de Montigny,[1] who were distinguished by their luxury, their regal packs and their debauchery. The Sire de Montigny, most of all, was typical of the lions of that era, in which blood reddened the tablecloths of orgies

---

1 Johan van Horne, Bishop of Liège (1450-1505) did indeed have two brothers, Frederik van Horne, Heer van Montigny (1450-1487), who was presumably his twin, and Jacob II, Graf van Horne, presumably his elder, who died in 1530 but whose birth date is uncertain. I have retained Joly's Frenchified rendition of their names.

as much as wine, in which ardent passions caused the law to fall silent at sword-point, and in which the spoils of a pillaged province, a city or a monastery were gambled on a throw of dice, to the cry of "Vive Bourgogne!" or "Vive France!" It was, therefore, the latter that Jean de Horne dispatched to the Castel d'Aigremont to relaunch a clandestine campaign against the grim wild boar that they dared not attack head on, so much did they fear his indomitable courage.

On a cold and foggy evening in the year of grace 1484, the archer placed at one of the stone sentry-posts overlooking the postern of the Château d'Aigremont hailed a group of cavaliers who had just stopped at the edge of the moat, after having considered with disappointed expressions the drawbridge whose extremity was touching the escutcheon forming the keystone of the arch of the postern.

"Hey!" cried the sentinel to the strangers. "Get away, quickly, or I'll send you a feathered bolt that will prove to you that there's only blows to earn here for mercenaries and Brabantines of your sort."

"The ribald fellow is well guarded," said a voice in the group outside, "and it'll do no good to attack him in his infernal burrow." Then, addressing the sentinel in a tone of imperious command, the same voice continued: "My lad, if you don't want to receive fifty good lashes on your ribs on my recommendation, go tell your lord and master that the Sire de Montigny, brother of the Bishop of Liège, his lord and mine, has come to ask for a night's hospitality, a flagon of Rhenish wine and a slice of venison. Go, and hurry."

The archer was heard to unload his arbalest, and his footsteps drew away inside the castle.

"Do you know, Monsieur, that it's tempting God to come and rest your head under the roof of that miscreant," said a voice other than the one that had called out to the archer.

"One can see by your courage, Messire Arnold, that you're a past master in reciting paternosters, not in feats of arms. We have nothing to fear from Messire d'Aremberg, who, might, after all, be less diabolical than he is said to be."

A sound of footsteps and voices came to interrupt that dialogue. The chain of the drawbridge was soon heard screeching, as it was lowered slowly on to the edge of the moat.

"Saint Lambert preserve us!" murmured Arnold. "We're about to find ourselves face to face with one of Satan's great barons."

"My brave and worthy pedagogue," said the Seigneur de Monigny, emphasizing each of his words, "If you'll take the advice of a beard less gray than yours, you'll hold your bridle and your tongue for as long as we're in this nest of vultures, and remember that one word or gesture might bring a host of the thieves swarming within down upon us, who would make a doublet out of their father's skin for a denier. So, be as prudent as a serpent and as silent as a carp."

Through the lowered portcullis they saw a group of men advancing armed with halberds and arquebuses; all of them wore a boar's head of red cloth on the right sleeve. Their harsh and grim features, illuminated by torchlight, contributed not a little to giving a physiognomy to the scene that was by no means reassuring.

"You want to talk to our master?" said a hoarse and drunken voice. "How many men compose your escort?"

"We are four: myself, my squire, my pedagogue and a page, all men little to be feared, having more inclination to play with jaws than knives, not to mention that we're as thirsty as lansquenets."

A nameless growl, which might have resembled a smile, responded to Montigny's speech, as he hastened to go through the portcullis, which had just been raised, as well as the bridge over the moat.

"Follow us, Monseigneur," said the man who appeared to be the chief of the night watch. I'll take you to my master."

On the heels of their guide, Montigny and his little retinue traversed a vast courtyard where grass grew thick and compact. The moon, from which a section of the veil of clouds had just drawn away, designed before them the black silhouette of an isolated tower in the middle of a vast courtyard. Shadows could be seen passing rapidly before windows illuminated with red and amber reflections, which seemed to be borne away by the whirl of some infernal waltz. A confused murmur of sounds and voices emerged from the vast hive of bandits, a cosmopolitan congress of cut-throats in which all people were represented by some rascal who had merited hanging three times over.

Montigny's guide went into the tower, climbed a spiral stairway hidden in the thickness of the wall, and then, pushing a door, went into the room from which the sounds audible in the courtyard were coming, telling his companions to wait there while he went to inform the Comte of their arrival.

The spectacle that struck the travelers' eyes was strange enough to merit their pausing momentarily, and, in spite of his audacity, Horne's younger brother felt somewhat troubled by the scene that was suddenly revealed to his sight.

Next to a vast hearth, under the immense mantel of which a few men, half-soldiers and half-brigands, were furbishing their morions and daggers, a few tables were placed, all occupied by gamblers in multicolored garments, which testified to the lack of concern their proprietors had for uniformity of costume. On the tables, vast earthenware pots and tinplate mugs passed by turns to the hairy lips of ruffians whose eyes were beginning to sharpen with the first gleams of intoxication. By their sides and in their belts shone weapons of every species, from the Frankish axe to the ultramontane stiletto.

Gold coins covered the heavy tables where dice clattered, each throw of which was accompanied by polyglot blasphemies and oaths. A few cleaned-out players, having become spectators, formed a gallery of virile, emphatic faces in which all the evil passions had left their imprints. A few paces from the gigantic fireplace, where the entire trunk of a beech was burning, a few dead-drunk mercenaries were lying, wrapped in their brown capes, whose snores rose up noisily in the rare moments of silence in which all breaths were suspended waiting for a decisive cast.

Each of the ruffians had conserved the distinctive characteristics of his nation; the Germans were getting drunk with a regal gravity, only interrupting their swigs to howl some bivouac song in chorus, with voices as hoarse and rusty as the tower's weather-vane; the French, the debris of the troop of three thousand men that de la Marck had amassed eight months earlier on the streets of Paris, which was composed of the cream of vagabonds, bad lots and the human filth that swarms around the by-ways of the Court of Miracles—that whole legion of lost children, avowed to the sword or the gibbet, on whom the war had levied such large tithes that only a hundred valid men remained—were singing carols and roundels at the tops of their voices, interrupted by joyful remarks and mad laughter.

From time to time, some loud threat would dominate the bacchanal; hands sought daggers and gazes a place to plant them; but a mysterious, inexplicable power prevent-ed the mercenaries from matching actions to words. It was vaguely sensible that upon those violent, sanguinary and unchecked natures, some mysterious influence weighed, which contained them and to which they submitted, while cursing it.

The walls of the vast hall, over which the flames of the hearth caused red and bloody gleams to run, were hung with weapons of war and hunting trophies—the antlers of stags, the heads of wild boar, the heads and skins of wolves—which the capricious games of the firelight caused to surge from the shadows like guests at some mysterious Sabbat. The entire strongly-characterized scene had struck the Sire de Montigny with some secret emotion, and per-haps he was repenting of having thrown himself impru-dently into the midst of that congress of bandits, some of whom were already looking curiously at the enormous gold chain suspended over his doublet, while others were communicating their observations in low voices.

An old lansquenet with a gray beard and a face like Cordovan leather labored with scars, doubtless taking Montigny for one of the recruits that the misfortunes of the times forced to have recourse to the agitated life of adventurers, said to him with a grotesquely paternal expression:

"You don't know, then, my lad, that thanks to the accursed peace of May last year, we've hung our daggers on the nail, and there are no more blows to strike since the death of Messire Louis XI, who gave us such good work during his blessed reign. Devil's horns! since the death of that protector of free mercenaries and barons of the green tent, here we are, wedged between Maximilien, Jean de Horne and the King of France like rats in the middle of a council of cats, without knowing where to go. Debauchery died with Charles de Bourgogne and Louis de Valois, may Satan's claw be light upon them! Become a cleric, lad, or, if your heart impels you, go be a warrior in Flanders. The good city of Ghent, which never remains tranquil for three months, will give occupation to your sword. As for us, we've become honest Christians; the Wild Boar hangs high and short anyone who steals a chicken from a peasant!"

"Ho ho! Listen to the Devil mounting the pulpit! The end of the world is nigh! Hermann, the old reiter, is preaching scorn for riches; the toothless old wolf is saying his paternosters."

The German's eye glittered with a flash of rage, and, seizing a heavy pewter tankard from the table he threw it at the head of the Parisian ruffian, who dodged the impact adroitly and drew his dagger in order to hurl it at his enemy. That was the signal for a terrible confusion; twenty daggers gleamed and a murderous ferocity was about to be unleashed when a velvet door-curtain suddenly moved aside and Guillaume de la Marck appeared.

At the sight of their redoubtable chief, whose severe gaze seemed to be demanding an account from them of that infraction of discipline, the mercenaries calmed down as if by enchantment and sheathed their daggers again with growls similar to those of a pack from whom a prey has been snatched away. The Sire de Montigny, who had witnessed the whole scene, which would have become bloody a moment later, advanced toward Comte Guillaume with a courteous and casual expression.

"Cousin," he said to him, "was I wrong to count on your courtesy and hope that you would accord us a night's hospitality in your manor? Our horses are exhausted and our stomachs empty; then again, the night is black and windy, and within an hour it will not be good to be out in the fields with no other shelter than a velvet doublet."

During that brief supplication, pronounced with a light nonchalance, de la Marck, who had initially taken on a cold and severe expression on seeing Montigny, abandoned the diplomatic gravity with which he had received his guest at first, and extended his hand to him with a harsh and military frankness.

"My château does not often have the pleasure of such visits, and it must require serious motives, Monseigneur, for you have forgotten that you have come to request hospitality of an outlaw that your family has too often tried to kill for me to have any illusion as to its sentiments in my regard. However, since you are my guest I shall treat you as such for as long as you care to honor us with your presence."

The solemnity of those words doubtless moved Montigny and made him think about the motive that had brought him to Aigremont, for, taking off his cape, which he was about to hand to a valet, he replied with an expression of apparent insouciance:

"Cousin, I've come to ask you for a slice of venison for me, litter for my horses, and shelter for us all, and here you are talking as if to an ambassador of my honored brother, come to propose a treaty to you. By the Holy Cross, treat me differently, I beg you. Affairs cause me to prick up my ears like an umbrageous horse. Everyone has his mission in this world. My honored brother and lord bishop will have sufficient credit in heaven, I hope, for me only to be sent to purgatory; as for myself, furry robes frighten me and I prefer good and rude companions like you who, drinking royally, know how to force a boar, cleave a helmeted head with a sword-thrust, handle a horse like a Moor and play for high stakes, without cursing if they leave their last château and ultimate doublet on the table."

After this fine profession of faith, whose principles had been put to work too many times by de la Marck for him not to welcome them favorably, Montigny planted his fist proudly on his left hip, turned up his moustache bravely and arranged his fringe as triumphantly as he could.

"By my beard, cousin," said de la Marck, nonplussed and bewildered by what he had just heard, "I'll be glad to see the proof if you practice your principles as well as you proclaim them."

Then, turning to Arnold, who had listened to that whole conversation with the air of a man who does not know whether he is awake or dreaming, he shook his hand rudely, saying to him with a smile that made the poor pedagogue tremble:

"You've made a pupil there who must not do you honor with the bishop, Messire. He'll be a good and proud soldier who will do honor to the flag under which he draws his sword. But that's enough talking, I'm forgetting that you need to fortify yourselves with something more solid than words. Follow me, sires, and may your appetite be equal to the supper."

"For that we can answer; the hunger of a Swiss and the thirst of a lansquenet are worthy of a king's table," said Montigny, unbuckling his sword, which he put under his arm.

Two ruffians as hairy as bears each took hold of a torch and preceded the Comte to the dining room, where a table was already set with a truly regal luxury. Arnold noticed, not without a secret alarm, that the cups destined for the guests were none other than chalices that the civil war and the looting of the Wild Boar's soldiers had caused to pass from monasteries and rich abbeys into the crenellated lair of the condottieri of Aigremont. The master's was enriched with precious stones and bore a golden relief representing the passion of Christ.

"Saint Lambert preserve us!" Arnold murmured in his master's ear. "This miscreant doubtless takes us for Saracens or Bohemians, to dare to offer us such cups."

Montigny's only response was to dart a thunderous glance at him while putting his index finger to his lips as a sign of discretion.

The supper commenced, splendid and abundant; the pages filled the vast cups that Arnold only lifted to his lips with dread; soon, however, the wine, key to all hearts and all secrets, illuminated the gazes of the guests. Montigny, who felt the need to conserve his reason intact, and was frightened by the vast thirst and gargantuan capacity of de la Marck, only lifted at rare intervals the vessel in which, with the gilded waves of Rhenish wine, all the goblins and fays of drunkenness were asleep.

"Oho, what's this? Are you saying thank you or asking for mercy?" exclaimed the Comte, darting a profound and inquisitive gaze at his guest.

"Until today, I've only seen cups of an honest size," said Montigny, picking up his golden vase, whose vast circumference would make today's drinkers—who fall asleep after the third bottle of champagne—shudder. "Unless one has Saint Anthony's fire in one's belly, I don't see a means of going beyond a few draughts; I thought I'd only have to empty two or three tankards, and you're proposing that I soak up the thunderstorms of Heidelberg; it's too much, in truth."

"Poor drinker, poor soldier," said the Comte. "That's the proverb."

"The proverb of a German or a sponge," hazarded Arnold, who was beginning to relax on seeing that the lightning had not come to trouble their supper.

"You can't always find life amusing in your falcon's nest," said Montigny, leaning back in his chair. "After an agitated life rich in excitement, like yours, the claustral solitude of your manor must weigh upon you. These vaults must stifle you, once always at war, sword in hand, driving a good horse into the heart of melees of steel and fallen enemies. Good God, you must get royally bored!"

"What would you do in my place, cousin?" said de la Marck, in whom the young man's words had caused the fire of battles to rise to his head. "Make war? Against whom? The peace of Arras has riveted all blades to their scabbards. Maximilien has let the house of Bourgogne fall under the fleshless hand of a royal cadaver who, on the edge of his tomb, has destroyed the great power of Charles de Bourgogne and Philippe le Bon. And then, today, to whom can one offer one's sword? I've learned from Louis de Valois what royal friendships are worth; has the wily colleague not ceded me bound hand and foot to Maximilien by his treaty of Arras? Have I not been paid with ingratitude by the Liègeois after liberating them from an insolent despotism? Go on! Gray beards like mine know what treaties and princely amities are worth. There's only one friend who has never deceived me thus far, and that's my sword."

"The solitude in which you live gives you these thoughts," replied Montigny. "Certainly, war has its pleasures, but peace has its delights. Why not come to Liège; there's more than one boar to force in the forests of Ardennes and more than one roe deer to bring down. Above all, there's more than one young gentleman who'd like to make his education in war under the lessons of your old experience. And then, the people love you in Liège, Messire, and sometimes mourn the times when the red boars led them against the enemy under the banner of Saint Lambert."

"The people love me, you say, cousin, but do the nobles and the clergy say as much? Have they forgotten that I broke in their hands the tyranny that Louis de Bourbon wanted to raise on the ruins of municipal liberalities? Is my name not an object of fear, a bloody flag that is not spared any infamy or atrocity? And can I respond with words of peace when every day the justice of a young madman throws the most beloved and respected heads on our antique perron? Can I be proud of sworn faith when the hand that had just posed on the Gospel signed death sentences two hours later, and sent the most trusting citizens to the gibbet? I've returned blood for blood, murder for murder, vengeance for vengeance, until they day when fatality or the demon placed Louis de Bourbon under my axe. And then, you see, there are misfortunes and crimes written on high."

With those last words, the Comte's forehead was covered by a dark cloud; one might have thought that a secret power, at that moment, was breaking that man of iron with indomitable passions. He took up his cup, and emptied it in one draught—and when he put it back on the table, the imprint of his teeth was visible thereon.

"To the Devil with these matters, and let's drink!" said Montigny, filling the cups. "The dead are dead and their marble armor is too thick ever to return them! To their health!"

Before Montingy's hand had reached his cup he felt it seized by the Comte, who, looking at him with a wild and terrible expression, hurled these strange words at him:

"Your words are those of a young man, cousin! Who has told you that marble tombs keep their remains icy and motionless? Who has old you that they don't awaken sometimes from their mysterious sleep to haunt the dreams of your nights and lean over your bed, pale and menacing, murmuring words that chill the bravest hearts with terror? Oh, enemies armed with steel, standing before you in the beautiful and joyful light of the sun, those at least the dagger and the sword are able to vanquish and kill—but what can those weapons do against the nameless beings that, icy and hideous by virtue of the contact of the tomb, come to lift the curtains of your bed, lie down beside you and soil you by their frightful contact, until the moment when cock-crow sends them back to their black and narrow prisons, where the worm, that crawling monarch of the tomb, quivers with joy at their arrival?"

The Comte had become animate during that strange sortie, in a feverish manner: his atonal and fixed stare seemed riveted straight ahead; his pale face, his bristling beard, and his clenched hands, which were mechanically tearing the velvet of his doublet, made his two guests shiver with fear, one of whom in particular—Arnold— was reciting under his breath some formula of diabolical conjuration.

"It appears that I don't have a fortunate hand in the matter of toasts," said Montigny, who pretended not to perceive his host's strange sortie. "Let's drink then, to some good war that will permit you to let your falcons fly, which you do not retain here, chaperoned, without difficulty. Good God! I thought a little while ago that I was going to witness some fine tourney in which the dagger replaced the lance! You must have given yourself a great deal of trouble, cousin, to discipline that rabble."

"Not too much," said the Comte, content to see the conversation turned away from a delicate subject. "When the Estates of Liège exiled me from my natal soil and chased me away like a toothless dog, I went to see King Louis, who received me in his Louvre and Plessis-les-Tours, a palace guarded by executioners, the rooms of which were jails where a legion of the damned howled behind its bars, in which Master Tristan[1] chose an ample tithe every day

---

1 The enigmatic Tristan l'Hermite, one of the most powerful men in Louis XI's court, was probably dead by the time Guillaume claims

for the royal oaks bordering the ditches of Plessis. I saw then the Phantom King whose fleshless hand could not have lifted a child's sword, but whose breath unleashed war over France, Germany, Burgundy and Flanders. At that time, his beautiful city of Paris was overflowing with vagabonds, Brabantines and other fiancés of the gibbet, who were giving fine work to the king's archers, killing bourgeois, abducting women, robbing shops in broad day-light, burning some warren of madwomen from time to time to distract themselves and liven things up a little, all ready to stab anyone for an écu and sell you their father for two. I therefore had it proclaimed in the city and on the parvis of Notre-Dame to the sound of the trumpet that all those who wanted to come and make war in Flan-ders and the land of Liège would find a gold mine there at the tips of their swords. That evening I counted three thousand, whom I dressed in beautiful red jerkins, and it was at the head of that flamboyant legion of demons that I forced the insolence of the estates of Liège to bow down before me."

"All that belongs to the past, cousin, and your persis-tence in keeping yourself shut away in your bastille and not taking account of the advantages and freedom of peace makes some people suspect your loyalty and convinces them that you're quietly preparing some savage attack in the provinces, and that one of these days you'll unleash your boars upon us. Now, wouldn't it be convenient to destroy those dangerous rumors by coming to share for a few days at the Episcopal palace the hospitality that you've so kindly offered to me?"

---

to have encountered him, but he also figures in Victor Hugo's *Notre-Dame de Paris*, set in 1482, and in *Quentin Durward*.

"They're saying in Liège that I want to start the war again! And who says that, Cousin?"

"Philippe de Clèves, among others."

"Philippe de Clèves is a liar, and by my beard, I'll come tomorrow to see you in Liège to show you that if I still want war, it's only against the tongues of serpents who have done more harm in the land than the blades of armed men. Now, cousin, let's go to bed, and tomorrow I'll go to show Philippe de Clèves that if de la Marck has sometimes shown himself proud and implacable to inflict just reprisals, at least he's never broken his sworn word."

Then, taking a silver whistle from his belt, he gave a known signal with it. Hermann immediately appeared at the door.

"Hermann, have ten men-at-arms ready at daybreak tomorrow to accompany me."

"Only ten men!" said the old mercenary, with an expression of surprise. "That's very few; the land is covered by Maximilien's troops and the communes are armed and organized everywhere in a fashion to rise up at the first summons of the belfry. If Monseigneur wishes, eighty horses can be readied as easily as ten, and will get the job done much sooner. All our men are hoping to get some air and take the rust off their swords.

De la Marck smiled, and, getting up from the table, approached the old reiter affectionately; then, taking him by his gray moustache, he said to him with a smile: "The time of good and appetizing expeditions is past, my old Hermann; today we're inoffensive canons, retired from business. So, ten horses as an escort of honor will suffice. Besides who will attack us in breach of sworn faith?"

"Who the Devil would think of attacking you?" said Montigny. "You have a renown for valor that is a shield in itself."

"There's no shield that protects from the dagger of a traitor," said Hermann, dully. "Besides, as I've observed to Monseigneur, many of our men desire to take the air, and I fear that . . ."

"What are you saying? Since when have their necks been itchy enough that they'd dare to disobey me?" said the Comte, arrogantly. "Carry out my orders and let all be said."

The old lansquenet went out with his head bowed, terrified by the flamboyant gaze of his master, which he knew to be the harbinger of some severe punishment.

"Your servants appear to love you a great deal," Montigny observed, with a pretence of sympathy for Herman's fears.

"There isn't one of them who wouldn't let himself be torn limb from limb ten times over rather than leave me in the hands of an enemy, all bodies of iron and hearts of bronze, lions in battle and after pillage. Where they've passed by, I defy the most voracious Jew to find anything to glean. And they're the men that Maximilien has rejected! Come the day when I can show at his expense what they're worth, though, and by my beard, he'll repent of it for a long time."

"Do you know, Cousin, that I'm very proud to have succeeded so well in my embassy?" said Montigny, placing his hand joyfully on the Comte's shoulder. "They're sure in Liège that you wouldn't dare set foot there, and now I'm bringing you back triumphantly to that noble and proud city, which has retained such profound memories of you.

Your presence there will reassure the minds that don't believe in the sincerity of the peace. We shall, in any case, render your sojourn in Liège agreeable: banquets, hunts, tourneys, nothing will be lacking, and if you please, I'll ask you, from this very evening, to be your brother in arms; for my pledge, I offer you my sword in exchange for yours, and tomorrow, at daybreak, we'll push on to Liège, where my noble brother will be very astonished to see his old but brave enemy!"

For his only response, de la Marck extended his rude but loyal hand to Montigny, and soon, in accordance with the custom of the Middle Ages, employed between brothers in arms, the same bed received them under its vast brocade curtains.

II

The following day, at dawn, ten well-mounted cavaliers chosen from the elite of the mercenaries were waiting for the master to appear in the courtyard of the manor of Aigremont, where old Hermann was maintaining, not without difficulty, the powerful neck of a proud horse. Soon, Montigny and the Comte appeared, and, leaping into the saddle, pushed their mounts toward the drawbridge.

At that moment a crow flew down from one of the crenellations in the ramparts and soared for a few seconds over the Comte's head uttering lugubrious cries. The sight of that messenger of misfortune, that sinister herald, uttering its raucous cries and covering the Comte with its ebon wings, cast some disturbance into the cavaliers. De la

Marck's reiters looked at one another with vaguely fearful expressions that contrasted with their martial allure.

Montigny wanted to break the charm that even appeared to be taking possession of the Comte, who, pensively, allowed the reins of his horse to hang loose while cocking an ear, as if he were seeking to divine the mysterious meaning of that warning.

"Good God!" he exclaimed. "If anyone had told me before today that the sight of a crow could sow fear among the proud soldiers of the Comte d'Aremberg and weaken the virile courage of their chief, I would have treated the man who had told me such a tale as a madman."

"Crows are prophets," said Hermann, interrupting Marigny. "At the battle of Blangy, one of those accursed birds came before the combat to glide, croaking, over the head of our commander, Gottfried, who did not fail to be one of the first killed. When they came to bury the dead, a bird in Satan's colors was found perched on the cadaver of the unfortunate captains. There's nothing to reply to that."

"There's this to say," said Montigny, who wanted to deflect the Comte's mind from the sinister presentiments that seemed to have taken possession of him, "which is that at the battle of Blangy there was a sufficient crop of blows struck with the sword, the arquebus and the axe for your captain Gottfried to have had his fair and honest share of them. As for the crow that was found on him, who can prove that it was the same one that had followed him before the combat? Your Germanic reveries are not common sense."

"Well, my old soldier, what will you respond to that?" said de la Marck, smiling. "Your belief in sorcerers, crows and marvelous presentiments is under attack"

"I've proved during the forty years that I've carried my skin through swords, bullets and crossbow-bolts in twenty battles that no one can suspect my courage," said Hermann in a somber voice, "but if such a warning from the heavens were given to me I would turn my bridle, convinced that some disloyal treason awaited me."

As he spoke these words, the old lansquenet had fixed his gray and piercing eyes on Montigny, whose embarrassment was visible momentarily. He soon collected himself, however, and, addressing the Comte with a grave expression, said in a tone of profound conviction:

"Sire Comte, I don't know to what extent your old servant's word might be true, but if that circumstance can give you any suspicion as to my loyalty, I'll return to Liège alone, not without regretting your determination."

A scornful and disdainful smile curved the lips of the Comte de la Marck; he turned in his saddle, cast a glance over his escort, looked at Montigny, and then at the fatal bird, which was still circling over his head with raucous cries; and finally, gripping his dagger convulsively and spurring his horse, he launched forward, shouting to his escort: "Forward, my boars, and to the Devil with Hermann and his crows!"

The old soldier muttered a few words into his gray moustache, promising himself mentally to leap at Montigny's head at the slightest circumstance that had an odor of treason.

The Comte and Montigny had taken the lead and, while causing their horses to exercise a thousand coquetries of equitation, continued to converse cheerfully. The thoughtlessness and frank gaiety of Montigny, who only talked about his brother the bishop and the most serious matters with a frivolous and insouciant levity, seemed to have driven any afterthought away from the mind of de la Marck—who, fundamentally, was not sorry to be extracted from the cold and tedious solitude of his manor of Aigremont and reentering somewhat into the active life for which he felt that he was made.

"By my beard," he said to Montigny, when the towers of Liège began to appear ahead of them, "the Liègeois will be very astonished to see their old friend again, who led them so often against the banners of the Bourbons and Bourgogne to the cry of 'Liège et Saint Lambert!' It's a good and old race, that of Liège, cousin, and it required nothing less than the combination of Burgundian and French knighthood to tame it and despoil it of its armor or ramparts. As long as my arrival does not lead to any popular noise."

"All that is forgotten today, cousin," said Montigny; "the French and the Burgundians have held out their hand and are only thinking of banqueting joyfully as often as possible. The clink of swords and breastplates has been replaced by that of tankards, and thank God, it's a beautiful and pleasant music better than that of battles!"

In fact, the arrival in Liège of the redoubtable mercenary whose feared banner had so often cast alarm into the hearts of the partisans of Louis de Bourbon, and which recalled terrible and bloody memories of the spring of Grivegnée—the unexpected circumstance of the abrupt appearance of a man whose turbulence and indomitable courage had maintained civil war for so long and curved beneath his despotism the most virile and proudest hearts of that city—was for the Liègeois an inexhaustible topic of commentaries, of which there was no lack.

The little troop, as it traversed the streets of Liège, did indeed almost provoke a riot, as de la Marck had feared. At the sight of their old chief and the fan-like red beard that covered his breastplate like a coat of arms, at the sight of the familiar red boars that ornamented the left sleeves of the doublets word by the reiters of Aigremont, an extraordinary emotion took hold of the Liègois, who soon formed an escort of men for the Comte that threatened to become an army.

Workers threw away their tools in order to come to salute the audacious rebel who had only ever been hard on the nobles and the rich, whose insolent pride he had broken, drowning their pretentions in a sea of blood. Women held up their infants in their arms to enable them to see the Comte, whose joyful gaze reposed on all the people who were throwing their hats and bonnets in the air with a thousand cries of: "Welcome to the good Sire de la Marck!"

The most ardent cleaved through the crowd in order to come and touch his weapons or his garments; those who could not reach him shook the hands of his men-at-arms, who smiled at them with a visible satisfaction. Only a few enraged Burgundians, returned since the peace, affected to keep their hats and bonnets, but the enthusiasm, too violent and too general, soon caused their headgear to leap into the air, and forced them, whether they liked it or not, to shout with the people.

"That's a reception of which a king would be proud, cousin," said Montigny, visibly annoyed by the ovation. "I've never seen these laborers as delighted and joyful; I don't know what's holding them back from carrying you and your horse in triumph, as they would a reliquary of

Monsieur Saint Lambert. By Our Lady, the peasants will deafen us with their cheers and cries of welcome! Some of them are howling like festival buccinas, and the crowd is flooding from all directions! If you'll take my advice, cousin, give your horse a thrust of the spurs."

In fact, the crowd was becoming so compact and urgent that it was necessary to make haste in order not to be imprisoned by the waves of the popular ocean. Animated by currents unfurling from the numerous somber streets of the city, de la Marck stood up on his horse and, in a thunderous voice that seemed made to dominate the din of battles, shouted:

"Thank you, children, for your good reception; I feared that you might have forgotten your old captain. Be moderate and prudent and don't spoil by your ardor the pleasure that I've come to seek among you. Now, comrades, a long and loud cheer for your prince Monseigneur de Horne."

The crowd, obedient to that voice, which had risen up of old to calm the lava of sedition, emitted a long hurrah, which made the windows of the bishop's palace vibrate as they arrived there.

"Cousin," said Montigny, half in jest and half in earnest, "I've never seen the Liègois welcome their natural lord in such a fashion. They have a furious love for you and a pleasant memory of the fine pillages to which you once led them."

"It's necessary that the amity of those worthy people console me somewhat for the hatred of the Burgundian bigwigs, who would like to see me swinging from a gibbet on the Pont des Arches. Good God, they had struck a bargain for my meat with Louis de Valois, who had already sold me and was getting ready to deliver me like a de-horned ram when Hermann's vigilance saw through that infernal plot. But what an excess of honor! His Highness the bishop coming to receive me himself, Cousin! This is one of those days that pour balm on the bitterness of past memories!"

Indeed, on the steps of the Episcopal palace, smiling and serene, stood Jean de Horne, followed by the servants of his house, some of whom came to help de la Marck descend from his horse. When he had set foot on the ground, Jean de Horne took a few steps toward him, holding out his hand with charming courtesy.

"Be thrice welcome in our good city of Liège, which has just shown you that it has retained a good memory of you. We thank you for having proven, by quitting your bastille at Aigremont and paying us this kind visit, that all rancor and memory of hatred are extinct between us. We ask you, for ourselves first and for our brothers the Comte de Horne and the Sire de Montigny, for a little of the good and loyal friendship that you will find in our house."

"As for us, we have already commenced," said Montigny, cordially. "The hospitality I received at Aigremont has made us brothers in arms, and we have exchanged our swords as a pledge of amity."

"If my presence here can be useful to you in the maintenance of peace," said de la Marck, "I pray Your Highness to believe that I shall deem myself glad to have been able to contribute to it. Bad advisers once provoked war between us; today, everyone has need of repose to repair the disasters of the war. The cities, like the armor of our soldiers, have experienced breaches to be plugged and damage to be mended."

After these words the bishop offered him his hand, and they both went up into the apartments of the palace, where de la Marck was treated with a royal magnificence. The exiled families who had returned to Liège since the peace of Arras rendered the sojourn at the Episcopal palace very agreeable. Every day brought new pleasures: hunts, feasts, balls, flights of falcons and nocturnal rides with the Sire de Montigny, who was striving to import to Liège, even to his brother's palace, the unrestrained mores and licentious pleasures of which Italy and Flanders were then the theater. The bishop's complaisance for his brother's excesses had already caused the Liègeois to murmur on several occasions.

The passions numbed in de la Marck during his sojourn at Aigremont were reawakened by that obsession and those temptations every day. Soon, he even frightened Montigny by his ardor for cruel sensuality. The demon of Grivegnée had reawaked in him, with all its old appetites for blood and vengeance. Sometimes, when wine, that diabolical counselor, held him in its power, his gaze had wild and terrible gleams that made his companions in debauchery tremble.

That existence, which suited de la Marck's energetic and passionate nature so well, lasted three entire months, during which more than one cadaver was thrown into the waves of the Meuse.

That comedy of amity was prolonged into the summer of 1485, until the moment of the catastrophe.

The town of Tongres was, along with Maestricht and Liège, one of the burgs in which the bishop exercised a part of temporal jurisdiction, and where the people, less well-disposed toward de la Marck than in Liège, permitted some treason against him to be enterprised without danger to the town's tranquility. The Comte de Horne, the Sire de Montigny and their companions in pleasure consequently assembled there in the month of June in order to spend a few days hunting.

On the eve of the departure, de la Marck was occupied in giving his instructions to his falconer when a valet came to tell him that the lansquenet Hermann was asking to speak to him.

"Let him come in," said the Comte, without disturbing himself.

The old soldier's attitude was anxious and embarrassed; his right hand was occupied in fondling the hilt of his dagger, while his left was turning his morion in the air with an expression of great confusion.

"What do you want with me, Herman?" said the Comte, full of good will. "Have you been so thirsty in recent days that you haven't a sou of your pay left, and have come to ask me for an écu to refresh your throat, paved with lava?"

"I've heard talk, Monseigneur, that you're leaving tomorrow for Tongres," said the German, sadly, looking at his master with an expression full of solicitude.

"That's true, my faithful friend. So what?"

"I'm also assured that you're departing with a crowd of cavaliers of the bishop's household, and thus alone in the midst of miscreants who are conspiring your doom."

"By my beard, Hermann, if they're conspiring my doom, it can only be in a manner to which you've adapted very well: balls, feasts, tourneys, always hunting, drinking, feasting and the rest, those are the means this miscreants are employing to get rid of me."

"In Bohemia, Monseigneur, when we want to catch a bear, we place a flayed sheep over a ditch covered with light branches, and the confident bear only finds instead of a prey, a hole in which pikes and arrows make short work of it."

"You've definitely emptied a few tankards too many today, Hermann; your brain has grown old and can no longer resist the fumes of wine. What are you telling me, with your bears, sheep and holes?"

"Since our departure from Aigremont, my mind hasn't been any more tranquil for having been able to drown in a jug of wine. But since you force me to explain, remember the crow of Aigremont and its sinister warning."

"A terrible presage, in truth, Hermann! Since we've been in Liège we've been marching from fête to fête, and without your sudden conversion, you'd have been able to compensate yourself here for your sojourn in Aigremont, which I head you curse so often!"

"I'm a Bohemian, Monseigneur, and my gray hair hides more wisdom than you suspect under my old cranium. Now, I say that I have seen the crow of Aigremont myself circling above your head, and your armor bearing on the raised collar a bloody golden fleece. Next to you was standing Bishop Jean de Horne, who seemed to be smiling at you with ferocious joy; as for you, Monseigneur, your face was pale, your beard soiled with traces of blood. I woke up troubled and exhausted, and I might perhaps have kept my terrors to myself if I had not learned this morning that you were about to quit Liège, where you can count numerous friends, to go to stay in a town entirely sat the discretion of the bishop, who must render you in hatred all the affection that his subjects have for you."

The Comte remained mute and pensive for a moment, and then, approaching his old servant, shook his hand affectionately.

"Your fears are foolish and unreasonable, Hermann. What reason could the bishop have to harm me? Would that not recommence a bloody war, when he has so much need of peace to consolidate his precarious power? In any case, to prove to you that I want to follow your advice, I'll have myself accompanied by a few of our old and redoubtable boars. Then, if you see anything that smacks of treason, warn me, and I'll soon prove to the traitors that my hand still knows where to find my axe or my sword."

The next day, the Comte de la Marck's escort, which had been joined by a large number of Episcopal men-at-arms and a crowd of lords, partisans of the bishop, departed for Tongres, where the Sire de Montigny was to meet his brother, the Comte de Horne. The adroit and cunning Montigny had been able, during the Comte's sojourn in Liège, to acquire such a firm grip on de la Marck's mind by throwing appropriate bait to his passions that the Wild Boar so no longer swore by anything but his faithful friend de Montigny, and marched with closed eyes toward the trap that had been prepared for him at such length.

On the twentieth of June, the bishop, to amuse and distract his guests and furnish his brothers with an opportunity to show their skill, hosted a pass of arms to which almost all the knights and gentlemen of the lands of Liège and Limbourg came. D'Aremberg and the Sire de Montigny declared themselves holders of the barrier against all comers and the chronicler from which we are borrowing our simple but faithful narration says that he "was marvelously wrought in feats of arms" that day.

After the passes of arms in which several morions were broken and many breastplates bruised, there was a great banquet in which de la Marck feasted abundantly on the exquisite wines that decked the bishop's table. Toward the end of the banquet, a jongleur came to ask to entertain the assembly with a few virelays.

"Let him come," said Montigny, already half drunk, "and if he amuses us, he'll have no cause for complaint."

"When these idle brayhards come to ask me for hospitality," said d'Aremberg, "I always have cause to complain of them; they're so well able to stir up my men that there's always some racket during their sojourn and some red rent in the doublet of one of my ruffians."

"Some of them know cheerful and joyous ballads of amour and drinking-songs; that's all we require of this one."

Although troubadours and minstrels were not as numerous in the fifteenth century, and their influence had declined greatly, France, Germany and Belgium especially still counted many minnesingers, whose boldness of thought had often made more than one insolent baron tremble and stopped more than one powerful prince in an unjust enterprise. Those heirs of Bertrand de Born always held with the same pride the scepter of opinion, flagellating crimes and ridicules in their naïve and energetic verses, at the risk of having no recompense but a solid rope attached to some seigneurial gibbet. Cherished by the people, whose plaints and hopes they translated, they found hospitality everywhere in thatched cottages and simple and faithful hearts, which venerated them with a naïve admiration.

The minnesinger, therefore, came into the banqueting hall at the moment when heads, lashed by the spur of wine, were as many volcanoes from which sprang strange, foolish, impious and atrocious words.

"Hola, companion, can you sing us the dictum of Renard, or that of the amorous monk, or some good and cheerful legend?"

"Such matters are not suitable for the ears that are listening to us, and I would have too much fear of injuring the respect due to His Highness the Bishop. I will sing you, if you please, the death of Roland at Roncevaux, of the treason to which the traitor Ganelon caused him to succumb, pitifully."

"You're nothing but a beaten donkey," said Montigny. "You don't know the most beautiful parts of your art. Sing us, then, whatever you wish, and above all, be careful not to send us to sleep."

The minnesinger commenced his virelay, to which only two persons were paying attention. D'Aremberg noticed that the singer's gaze fixed itself on his when he pronounced the name of Roland, and reported with a marked affectation to Montigny when he unfurled the treasons and black machinations of Ganelon. The bishop was only occupied in filling d'Aremberg's cup, which he emptied mechanically without appearing to have any consciousness of what he was doing.

"May Saint Anthony's fire rack your Ganelon and your Roland," said Montigny, whom the minstrel's intention had visibly troubled. "You're only good for putting drunken monks to sleep. Your song has neither gaiety nor interest."

"I beg Your Nobility's pardon," said the minstrel,

resting his gaze on d'Aremberg. "It proves that neither strength, nor valor, nor any weapon, no matter how well-tempered it might be, can prevail against hidden weapons poisoned by treason, and that if Roland, the famous paladin, succumbed by virtue of the endeavors of a traitor, there is no one who can believe himself strong enough to fight against enemies who emerge from the shadows at the moment when his hand and sword repose on the faith of a false and disloyal amity."

D'Aremberg had gone pale; his hand had gone mechanically to his dagger, and his gaze seemed to be interrogating the slightest suspect gesture in order to plant it straight in the heart of Montigny and the bishop. Whether it was the revelation of a good angel or one of those sudden enlightenments that sometimes tear the veil of mist that drunkenness casts over thought, a somber mistrust seemed to take possession of him, and, pushing away the glass that the bishop presented to him with joyful invitation, he summoned the singer to approach him.

"Come here that I might repay you for your beautiful song, friend. Here, take this chain, and add to your song that if Roland had only had to combat a handful of damsels clad in silk, through which the blade of a dagger would have frayed a facile passage, he would not have remained lying beneath the rocks of Roncevaux. Now take this silver cup, drain the wine and keep the metal for the bad days when your song of Roland will not bring you anything."

The minstrel bowed and went out, not without having cast a profound and significant gaze upon the Comte.

At the corner of a street the minnesinger was ardently accosted by Hermann the lansquenet.

"Well?" said the soldier.

"You can see by this chain that he understood me," said the singer. "Nevertheless, I fear that a cup of that ensorcelled wine might render him a dangerous confidence."

"May God grant you a Christian death," said Hermann, "but every moment that goes by augments my dread. A company of two hundred crossbowmen has just arrived. Everything is in movement around the bishop's palace. Death of my life! If a single hair falls from my master's beard, I swear to disembowel every last member of that accursed bishop's race! In any case, I'm beginning to believe that we've fallen into an infernal wasps'-nest. The bishop's soldiers are looking at us in a fashion that doesn't presage anything good. And there's no means of warning the Comte overtly! His violence will doom him; he'll stab one of those dandies, perhaps even the Bishop, and we'll be no further forward. It's necessary to try to get out of here without awakening suspicions; to attempt it be force would put us at odds with three hundred men-at-arms and an entire population. Oh, why didn't the Comte want to understand me?"

The departure of the minstrel and the impression he had left on the bishop's guests had chilled the joyful gaiety that had animated the party. De la Marck, his elbows on the table, was parading his gaze over all those surrounding him; an implacable and savage rage seemed to be brooding within him, only waiting for a word or a gesture to burst forth. At that moment he resembled the living animal that he had taken for a blazon, so ferocious and haggard was his expression.

"May the quartan fever grip the blackguard who has come to cast clouds over our joy," said Montigny. "Here we are, as pensive and bored as monks at matins in winter! With that, one last toast to our good friendship, Messeigneurs, and may the first who breaks it have ergotism and bitter wine to appease his thirst!"

D'Aremberg raised his cup, but on seeing so much gaiety and abandonment on the faces that surrounded him, he blushed at his suspicions and emptied it in a single draught.

At that moment a valet came into the room carrying a large box made of precious wood in his arms, which he set down before the bishop.

"Cousin," said the bishop, placing his hand on the lid, "we wanted to prove our amity to you by treating you as a brother, in welcoming you to our pleasures and all our dalliances. Today we want to beg you to accept a gift from our own hand, which would not be out of place on the shoulders of a king."

As he spoke, the bishop took out of the box a brocade robe of purple silk damascened with gold, which he displayed to the eyes of the assembly, amazed by such a truly royal present.

"Come here, valiant and handsome cousin, that we might present our pledge of amity personally."

The Comte, confused by the suspicions that Hermann's envoy had succeeded in engendering within him, approached the bishop, who put the robe over him with a gracious courtesy.

"And now that peace is reestablished between us," Montigny said to d'Aremberg, taking his hand, "let's go liven things up a little and try your horse, of which you're so proud. I'll wager a hundred gold écus that you won't overtake me in a race over the distance of a league."

"One can see, cousin, that you only have to roll up the sleeves of your doublet to draw upon the Episcopal purse," said d'Aremberg, with an ironic smile. "Nevertheless, I accept your challenge—but where are we to carry it out? The road from Tongres to Liège is scarcely favorable. It's bad enough to break the bones of a Christian and a horse twenty times over before reaching the end of the course."

"So it isn't that abominable road, as rude and difficult as the one to paradise, that it's necessary to choose, Cousin. The one from Tongres to Maestricht is good, easy and well-maintained, thanks to our honored brother's gangs of laborers."

All the guests left the room in order to get ready to watch the race, which offered the keenest interest. The Comte de la Marck's horse, to which Montigny had alluded, was a superb and vigorous animal given to the Comte by King Louis XI, the most magnificent prince of Christianity when it was a matter of attaching a partisan or winning over an enemy. De la Marck was also reputed to be one of the most intrepid horsemen of his era. Hermann soon brought his master's charger, whose proud allure and vigorous appearance presaged Montigny's defeat. The old soldier also held his master's sword, heavy and massive, a veritable battle-sword. He presented it to the Comte with a bleak and resigned expression.

"What do you want me to do with this, Hermann?" said the Comte, rejecting the weapon, which bore many deep notches on the hand-guard. "In a horse race, a sword is an unnecessary and harmful thing, which only serves to embarrass the rider and frighten his mount. Take it away, or, if you want to follow me, keep it for me until after the race."

The old lansquenet took back the sword without saying a word, and went to get his horse, which he mounted, murmuring: "It's his destiny, and the crow of Aigremont was right."

The riders had reached the gate of Tongres, where, while discussing the conditions of the race, the bishop and his brother, the Comte de Horne, went on ahead in order to be able to judge the arrival and make sure that no obstacle was to be found on the road.

After a quarter of an hour, all the arrangements had been made and the adversaries were ready to depart at the first signal. Hermann approached the Comte under the pretext of adjusting his horse's girth-strap and whispered a few words into his ear.

"Turn the bridle and let's ride full tilt away from these Judases; once away of Tongres, we'll be safe!"

De la Marck shrugged his shoulders and, turning his head toward the Sire de Ravenstein, who was to give the signal, shouted that he was ready.

"Then be alert, Messeigneurs," said Ravenstein, "and set off at the signal of the gunshot." Then, raising an enormous pistol into the air, he shouted one last time: "May God protect you, Messires!" and fired.

A cloud of dust suddenly raised up prevented the two cavaliers from being perceptible for some time, until they surged forth from the dusty whirlwind two hundred meters further on, racing side by side, leaning over the necks of their mounts, which seemed to be devouring distance. All gazes followed them until an abrupt bend in the road hid them from view.

Meanwhile, the Comte de la Marck gradually gained ground on his adversary by virtue of the superiority of his horse, which followed, as rapidly as thought, the road that seemed to be fleeing beneath its four agile feet. Soon, the Comte found himself alone; the road was deserted—except that behind him a little cloud of dust indicated all the terrain that his competitor had lost.

In that epoch the road from Tongres to Maestrcht was nothing but a broad pathway, hollowed out through the densely wooded thickets that succeeded one another at brief intervals all the way to Maestricht. The road snaked, so to speak, between two somber and bushy curtains of verdure.

D'Aremberg stopped his horse abruptly in order to cast a glance ahead of him to see whether he might be able to perceive the end of the course, where the bishop and his brother, the Comte de Horne, ought to be stationed. He interrogated the horizon vaguely, but nothing was visible. A vague presentiment gripped him; he put a hand to his belt to make sure that his dagger was not too tight in its sheath; then, looking down at his steaming horse, he was about to resume his course when a sound that became audible in the foliage made him turn his head. Twenty arbalestiers were lying in ambush. At the same moment, the thicket opened in front of him and fifty arquebusiers, their wicks lit, with the Comte de Horne at their head, cut off the road that extended before him.

De la Marck darted a rapid glance backwards, which made him understand that his situation was utterly desperate. His beard bristled; his pale lips and bloodshot eyes testified that the storm was about to burst. The archers and the arequbusiers, mute and motionless, still held their weapons aimed at his breast, which was only defended by a simple silk doublet.

The Comte de Horne, sword in hand, prey to an emotion that made him tremble, followed de la Marck's every movement with his eyes. D'Aremberg, like a true wild boar surrounded by a furious pack, slowly turned in that circle of death to seek a means of breaking out. It was a supreme moment.

Suddenly, a dusty cavalier pierced the arbalestiers and cried, in a breathless voice: "Well, is the boar caught?"

De la Marck roared like a wounded tiger, and, as rapid as lightning, hurled himself at the cavalier, who was none other than Montigny, and before the latter could anticipate his design, struck him in the breast with such a furious dagger-thrust that the weapon broke with a loud snap, just as Montigny was about to measure the earth with his entire length.

"You haven't counted on my good coat of mail lined with leather, cousin," said Montigny, with an ironic expression. "But, by God, since we finally have you where we've desired you for a long time, it's necessary to pay for that joy with some trouble." Then, addressing himself to the archers, who seemed indecisive: "Tie him on to his horse, and at the first sign of rebellion lodge twenty bullets in his accursed skull."

Resistance having become futile, de la Marck submitted without trying to carry a struggle without result any further. Still ignorant of what they wanted of him, he did not want to run from a certain death. Meanwhile, he approached the two brothers de Horne; after having contemplated them with mortal scorn, he spat in their faces.

"You're the peers of Judas the apostle who kissed his master on the lips before delivering him! Gentlemen with neither courage nor loyalty—give me weapons, and if within an instant I don't lay you both in the dust at my feet, I'll consent to die like a criminal at the end of a rope." To the archers surrounding him, he said: "Soldiers, in whatever place you see the banner of the Hornes, remember that it is that of cowards and traitors, who need nothing less than an army to capture a single man!"

"Did you think, then, that the murder at Grivegnée would remain unpunished and that the blood of Louis de Bourbon would be unavenged?" said Montigny, with an infernal smile. "You were able to defy human justice while you were sheltered behind your walls and defended by your legion of brigands and outcasts, but when one cannot kill a wild boar in its stronghold, one drives it into the plain, where one gives it short shrift, as you shall see. Your insolent fortune should have warned you of your end. You have forced the city of Liège to exhaust its treasures for you, to give you its most beautiful châtelaines; you reigned there for two years like a highwayman, casting into the Meuse or to the iron of your brigands everyone who did not bow down before you, and you thought that Satan would protect you until the end! Ha ha ha!"

"You are cowards," shouted de la Marck, in a deafening voice, "and my blood will splash your dishonored blazon with an ineradicable stain. Now, hasten to deliver my neck to the executioner, for centuries to come, because, by my beard, you have made me take life and men in disgust!"

The arquebusiers approached the Comte with a visible sentiment of respect for such a great misfortune, and having tied him to his horse, covered his head with a large floppy hat, which prevented his features from being distinguished; then, quitting the highway, they took winding paths and arrived that evening in Maestricht, where Bishop Jean de Horne had made all the preparations to receive his prisoner.

De la Marck was taken to the Episcopal prison, where he was guarded by the bishop's men and a few armed burgers of the town. The bishop spent part of the night assembling a simulacrum of a tribunal before which the prisoner was taken. In the morning, they were obliged to wake de la Marck up by telling him that his judges were waiting for him.

"My judges," he said, "are unnecessary; there's only need to send for the executioner." However, he soon got up and followed his jailer, who led him to the bishop's room.

Jean de Horne was sitting on an elevated armchair, surrounded by a few burgomasters and the mayor of Maestricht. A clerk was stationed beside the bishop, ready to write down the Comte's replies. The latter, after having paraded a proud glanced over all that magistracy hungry for his blood, threw himself on to the seat that had been prepared for him.

"Guillaume d'Aremberg Lumey de la Marck, you are accused, firstly, of having treacherously murdered on the thirtieth of August 1482, at the Moulin de Wez near Grivegnée, your lord and benefactor Louis de Bourbon, bishop of Liège; secondly, of having wickedly pillaged, desolated and tyrannized our good city of Liège, of which you had yourself named mambour by violence; and finally of having broken the sworn peace of Arras by making excursions and pillaging monasteries on the lands of Brabant. What have you to respond?"

"Nothing, except that you ought to conclude your infamous comedy as soon as possible," said de la Marck. "Every time I had to hang someone, I never bothered amusing myself by judging him."

The bishop turned to the clerk, tranquilly. "Write that the accused here present before us confesses his crimes and that he is in haste to arrive at the moment of expiation." Then, addressing the archers guarding the Comte, he said to them: "Take the prisoner away, until we have decided his sentence."

D'Aremberg followed his guards meekly with an astonishing resignation; he had no further illusions as to his fate.

"As long as they finish it soon," he said to one of the Bishop's officers, "for after a day so full it's permissible to take a little repose." Then, as if reminiscing, he continued with a cheerful insouciance: "This morning, a tournament of arms, then a banquet, a horse race, all the joys; this evening, to close a day so well commenced, judges, and tomorrow a block and an executioner."

Half an hour passed thus in waiting. The voice of the Bishop was heard, which seemed to be speaking with a great deal of fire; then, moments later, the door opened and the clerk made a sign to the soldiers to bring in the prisoner.

When de la Marck reentered the hall of justice, the Bishop was pale and agitated, and his gaze seemed to avoid that of his victim. The burgomasters seemed confused and embarrassed. Finally, the clerk read the prisoner a long and confused sentence that concluded with the prisoner's condemnation to death, which warned him to prepare for it the following day at sunrise. After that reading, the Bishop asked the prisoner whether he had anything to say or to request.

"I have to say," de la Marck replied, "that I have committed many sins and many crimes in my life as a soldier, but I believe them sufficiently expiated by the horrible death that you are preparing for me. I also have to say that my blood, which you are about to shed with so much scorn at this moment, will weigh heavily upon your death-bed, Sire de Horne—and on your consciences, Messires," he added, addressing the trembling judges. "As for my desires, in my situation the only one that one ought to form is that the executioner be adroit and that the axe cuts cleanly!"

On the Place d'Armes in Maestricht, at the place where the Hôtel du Casque stands today, the bishop's scaffold then stood. It was a great pillory in blue stone, at the base of which was the block destined for executions. The whole was surmounted by the armories of the bishop and the city of Liège. Six or eight steps led up to that scaffold, which was visible from the bishop's palace.

At five o'clock in the morning, the archers came to fetch de la Marck in order to take him to the place of execution, and were astonished to find him profoundly asleep. He received those messengers of death very meekly, had them comb his long beard, of which he had always taken the greatest care and by which he was accustomed to swear. The barber charged with that task had completed his work when a colossus dressed in a leather doublet came in, who asked de la Marck rudely if he counted on keeping his beard.

"What has that to do with you, peasant?" said the Comte, proudly.

"It's just, you see, Monseigneur, that it might harm my reputation, cause the cutlass to deviate, and that I'd be sorry if any misfortune befell you."

"Oh, I understand, then; it is your province. However, if the thing can be done without cutting my beard, the old banner that has made the Burgundians and the bishop's bloodhounds flee so many times . . . what do you think, friend?"

"If Your Lordship will promise me to hold it in his teeth during the execution, everything can be arranged," said the man.

"By God, that's a good idea!" said the Comte. And, gathering up the vast fan that covered his breast, he compressed it in such a manner as to be able to hold it in his teeth.

"That's it," said the man. "Now, let's go."

"One more word," said the Comte. "The garments of the condemned belong to you. Now, for a particular reason, I don't want to be separated from this robe of red damask; it as a last gift from the bishop, who gave that bloody shroud to me personally this morning. Swear to let me keep it—here's three golden écus to compensate you."

The executioner swore on his children, and the prisoner set forth.

A sea of heads was undulating on the Vrythof, and from that ocean of men not a single sound went up. The sun was casting its joyous and fresh morning rays upon the scaffold, above which flocks of birds were passing, uttering their joyous cries. Soon, the balcony of the palace was seen to open, and the Bishop and his two brothers appeared, all as pale as the damned. A muted murmur of the people did justice to that final cowardice.

A moment later, the crowd opened before the halberds of archers and de la Marck appeared, his head held high, covering the crowd with a long and supreme gaze. He climbed the steps of the scaffold slowly, and looked at all the apparatus of his death with the greatest calm. Then, having turned toward the palace, his eyes radiated a savage hatred.

The three de Hornes were there, watching his last hour and savoring their enemy's anguish. The entire people understood what was passing through the soul of the condemned man, and began to boo the bishop, who remained impassive, doubtless not wanting to miss any of the emotions of the Comte's torture.

Finally, the latter shrugged off his robe, gathered his beard into his mouth, and placed his head on the block.

At that moment, a flock of crows took off from the towers of Saint Servais and came to utter lugubrious croaks above the crowd.

The Comte raised his head, followed the black heralds of death with his eyes for a time, and then replaced it on the block, which soon resounded with a blow so terrible that the head, leaping from the scaffold, went to bounce into the crowd, which opened before it with a cry of horror. The executioner went to pick it up; the clenched teeth were gripping the long beard with such force that it could not be taken out of his mouth.

While returning from Maestricht to Liège, following that beautiful expedition, the bishop and his two brothers were traveling tranquilly when the blast of an arquebus was heard and a bullet lifted off the Sire de Montigny's velvet bonnet. Near Herstal, a second bullet came to kill one of the bishop's officers who was marching beside him. The peasants affirmed that they had seen a man running away, whom Montigny recognized as Hermann, the lansquenet.

No one knew for a long time the location of the sepulcher of Guillaume de la Marck, the Wild Boar of the Ardennes; then, in the eighteenth century, while repairs were being made to the Dominican church in Maestricht, a lead coffin was discovered containing a cadaver clad in a red brocade robe; the head, separated from the body, was recognizable by the prominence of the maxillary bones and the length of the beard that filled the entire capacity of the mouth.

We have had in our possession a piece of that red brocade robe given by the bishop to the Wild Boar of the Ardennes, which became his shroud; it has been shared out between several individuals and transmitted preciously from father to son. It is from one of those descendants that we have the authentic information that we have just imparted, and which has been extracted from a manuscript almost contemporary with the death of that extraordinary man, whose end was a bloody expiation but will be an eternal stain on the name of de Horne.

OTHER SNUGGLY BOOKS YOU WILL ENJOY ...

BLUE ON BLUE
by Quentin S. Crisp

A SUITE IN FOUR WINDOWS
by David Rix

NIGHTMARES OF AN ETHER-DRINKER
by Jean Lorrain

DIVORCE PROCEDURES FOR
THE HAIRDRESSERS OF A METALLIC AND
INCONSTANT GODDESS
by Justin Isis

BUTTERFLY DREAM
by Kristine Ong Muslim

GONE FISHING WITH SAMY ROSENSTOCK
by Toadhouse

THE SOUL-DRINKER
AND OTHER DECADENT FANTASIES
by Jean Lorrain

MENDICANT CITY
by Yarrow Paisley

THE OUTCAST SPIRIT AND OTHER STORIES
by Lady Dilke

CLARK
by Brendan Connell